Bitter Taste of Love

A Novel

Stacey Covington-Lee

Published by Delphine Publications

ISBN: 978-0989090629

Edited by: Tee Marshall
Layout: Write On Promotions
Cover Design: Odd Ball Designs
Printed in the United States of America

Bitter Taste of Love

PROLOGUE

Cecily laid in the bed with tears rolling down her face. This room was where she felt comfortable. The man that lay beside her was the one that made her feel wanted, desired, and loved. It was hard for Cecily to accept that this would be their last night together. To leave Carter was not what her heart, her soul ached for. Instead, every fiber of her being begged her to stay with him for the rest of time. But Cecily had decided to follow her mind and it told her to return home. Home to her babies and to the farce that was her marriage to Andrew. This decision was proof that there were no lengths too far for a mother to go in order to secure a good future for her children.

Carter turned over in bed. Even in the darkness of the night, he could see the pain etched in Cecily's face. "Love, why are you crying?"

"Because it's just so hard to accept that this is our last time being together. You've become such an important part of my life and now I have to let you go. The thought of being without you hurts so badly. I mean it physically hurts, baby. I don't know how I'm going to make it through this."

"I told you, Cecily, this is not the end for us. I refuse to accept that you won't be a part of my life anymore."

"But Carter..." Before Cecily could finish her thought, the bedroom door was damn near kicked off of its hinges. No words were spoken; the only sound was that of bullets being released into the shadows of the night.

CHAPTER 1

Cecily looked around the house in disgust. She'd spent the day before making sure that the house was spotless, food was in the refrigerator, and clothes were cleaned, pressed, and hanging in the closets. She had planned a girls only weekend at one of the downtown hotels and wanted to make sure that her family had all they needed before she left. But less than twenty-four hours into her much needed get-away, Andrew called insisting that she return home immediately. One of the kids was sick and needed her mother. When she arrived at the house, the kids were with a babysitter and Andrew was nowhere to be found.

Irritated with the situation, Cecily yanked out her phone and dialed Andrew's cell number. "Where are you?"

"Hey babe, a couple of the guys were getting together for a few rounds of golf and called me to come hang with them."

"You mean to tell me that you interrupted my weekend, which was planned weeks ago, so that you could go play golf? What the hell, Andrew?"

"Look, they're waiting on me. You know I don't know what to do with a sick kid so just handle it."

"Handle it! She has the sniffles. I left her medicine and the schedule for which it was to be given. Was that really too much for you to handle?"

"Bye, Cecily." The next thing she heard was a dial tone. Cecily was furious. This was typical behavior for Andrew, always thinking of no one but himself.

Cecily took a few deep breaths, stood to her feet and looked around. It appeared as if a tornado had hit the kitchen and family room. She closed her eyes, waited a few seconds and opened them again in hopes that the house would've magically cleaned itself. When that didn't work, she went to the basement, paid the babysitter, and ordered the kids to their rooms for work detail. Returning to the kitchen, she began to clean it and the rest of the house all over again.

The remainder of the day was spent catering to the kids. They had story time at the library, dinner and games at Stevie B's, and finally her babies were tucked into bed and sleeping like a couple of rocks. Now it was time for Cecily to have a moment to herself. She was hoping to enjoy a long, hot bubble bath and glass of wine before Andrew made his grand entrance.

It was 1:30a.m. and Andrew still wasn't home. Cecily lay in bed, remote in hand, flipping television channels. She wondered what kind of ball game he was really participating in because it certainly wasn't golf. She finally settled on some show about athlete's wives. The longer she watched the program, the more she was convinced that a couple of the women needed therapy. She couldn't understand why the women put up with the behavior of the men, or other women for that matter. It was simply ridiculous. Were they really willing to deal with such foolishness in exchange for living high on the hog? Then it hit her like a ton of bricks. She was no better than they were. Maybe they could get a group discount on the therapy. There she was lying in a bed looking around at the nicely decorated room and realizing that she was in the coldest room of the house. There was no love, no warmth, and no passion in that room. It was simply a place to lay her head. The realization sent a single tear on a journey down her cheek.

Two hours later Andrew came creeping in the house. Cecily didn't move, she just quietly watched him as he removed his clothes and crawled into bed. The idea of being face-to-face with him nauseated her and she immediately turned her back to him. As if that were some type of invitation, Andrew moved in closer and wrapped his arm around her waist. She tried to pull away but he used his strength to draw her back.

"Andrew, let me go. I don't want you touching me."

"You're my wife, touching is what we're supposed to do. Now come on and make me happy, babe."

"I said let go!" Cecily scrambled to get out of bed, but Andrew pulled her back. This time he was little more forceful and Cecily knew that if she didn't go along with it, he would make life a living hell. She closed her eyes and laid there, an unwilling participant while he had his two minutes of ecstasy.

CHAPTER 2

By mid-week, Cecily was beginning to feel more sluggish than usual. She had threatened to go to the doctor a couple of times but hadn't made good on them. Instead, she continued to push herself. The children had to be cared for, the house had to be maintained, and her job wasn't going to work itself.

Cecily and Andrew had decided that it would be best for her to give up her career as an account manager for a prestigious firm and stay home full time once their son, Brian was born. It was always Cecily's plan to return to work once Brian was old enough for Pre-K. It just so happened that she discovered she was pregnant again two weeks before Brian's fourth birthday. It was her tough luck that she was among the one percent of women that the pill didn't work for. Rachel was indeed a blessing, but Cecily had thought it would be easier to start over as a single mom if she only had one child.

Now that Rachel was four years old and able to tell if anyone bothered her, Cecily decided to return to work. She realized years ago that she couldn't depend on Andrew for anything except the bare necessities. It was true that he paid the mortgage and utilities. But anything above and beyond that, Cecily was on her own. The kids had all that they needed and most of what they wanted while she made do with what she already had. Occasionally, Andrew would feel generous enough to let her purchase a new dress or get her hair done, but those times were few and far between. Cecily hadn't worked hard to earn her Masters Degree in order to be some man's underpaid and unappreciated maid.

Cecily always made it a point to take the stairs at work, but today she was not able. Her body was tired and she could not muster the energy. She pressed the up button on the elevator, stepped in, and leaned against the wall for the brief ride. As soon as she made it to her desk, she pulled out her phone and dialed her doctor's office.

"MedCare, may I help you?"

"Yes, this is Cecily Connors. I need to make an appointment with Dr. Stanford."

"I can get you in next week, Mrs. Connors. Which day works best for you?"

"Is there any way I can get in this week, maybe an emergency appointment?"

"Well, we do have one cancellation for tomorrow at 8:45a.m. I know that's pretty early but it's all we have for this week."

"I'll take it."

"Alright, Mrs. Connors, we'll see you in the morning."

"Thank you."

Cecily disconnected the call, pulled herself to her feet and made her way to her manager's office. "Mr. Richardson, do you have a second?"

"Sure Cecily, what can I do for you?

"I'm not feeling my best, is it okay if I take off for the rest of the day and come in late tomorrow? I have a doctor's appointment first thing in the morning."

"No problem, we can hold the fort down without you for a while. Do what you

need to do and feel better soon."

"Thank you, I'll see you later tomorrow."

Cecily gathered her things and headed for the door. As she drove across town, she

thought about how thankful she was that she would have a couple of hours to rest before the kids would have to be picked up from school. It wasn't long before she pulled into the garage, made her way through the house and up to her bedroom. She pulled out her cell phone and set the alarm for an hour and a half later. Then Cecily collapsed across the bed and was sleep in a matter of seconds.

The alarm went off and Cecily slowly rolled over. She pulled herself up, grabbed her things, and left to pick up the kids. On the way back home, they took a vote on what they would have for dinner. It would have to be fast food because Cecily did not have the energy to prepare a home cooked meal. Thankfully the kids settled on KFC without too much of an argument. As soon as they got into the house, Cecily fed her babies, helped with homework and got them ready for bed.

"Mommy, can we stay up and wait for Daddy. We want to tell him goodnight," Brian whined.

"Sweetheart, Daddy is working late. If you're still awake when he gets home, I promise to let you get back up and speak with him. Okay?"

"Okay."

Cecily walked each child to their room, gave them sweet hugs and kisses, and bid them a goodnight. With the house calm and quiet, she headed for the shower, and then poured herself back into bed. She was anxious for morning to arrive and desperate for answers about why she was feeling the way she was.

An hour into her peaceful state of rest, Cecily was jolted awake by the sound of the garage door going up. She hated that damn garage for the noise that it made. It was

right underneath the master bedroom and was notorious for creating the foulest sound imaginable. As the door went back down, Cecily tried to hurry and fall back asleep. Andrew had a knack for knowing when she was faking sleep and Lord knows she did not want to be bothered with him tonight. But it seemed like only seconds before he walked into the bedroom and her body had failed to surrender to sleep.

"Hey, it's kind of early to be in bed, isn't it?"

"I haven't been feeling my best today. Thought I'd call it an early night. How was your day?"

"It was a day. You've been complaining a lot lately. What's wrong with you *this time*?"

"Wow, Andrew, you sound so concerned."

"I am concerned. But like I said, you've been complaining a lot. How ill can one person be? Was there any dinner left?"

"There's a plate in the microwave." Cecily snapped as she rolled back over and pulled the covers over her head.

Snatching the covers back, Andrew asked, "What is it?"

"It's KFC, now leave me alone."

"Baby, come on. I've been working hard and all I have to eat is some cold fast food? Can't you at least fix me something simple but good real quick?"

"What part of 'I'm not feeling well' didn't you understand? Now let the covers go, I'm cold."

"Come on, baby, just some scrambled eggs, bacon, and toast. Now that's fast and you'll be back in bed in no time."

"Andrew, we both know damn well that if the tables were turned you would not get out of bed to cook for me. And why can't you understand that I don't feel well?"

"I understand that you are in bed at 8:30. Looks like you're just lazy as hell. If you were as sick as you claim to be, you would've made your way to a damn doctor by now."

"I have an appointment in the morning, Andrew."

"Well good for you, now come on and fix me something to eat…please."

Knowing that she would not have any peace until he was satisfied, Cecily dragged herself out of bed and headed downstairs to the kitchen. She was so angry; the neighbors could have probably heard her throwing pots and pans around. Cecily threw some bacon in the microwave, bread in the toaster, and cracked two eggs open over a hot skillet. She didn't care how this crap tasted, to be honest, she was trying to purposefully make it taste like garbage. When she was done, she sat the plate on the table with a glass of cranberry juice.

"Andrew, your food is ready." Cecily bellowed without any regard for her sleeping children. Thankfully they did not wake up.

Andrew came bouncing down the stairs as Cecily was trying to make her way back up. "Now see, baby, that didn't take you but a hot minute."

"I hope you choke on it," she mumbled.

"What did you say?"

"I just said goodnight. Please try and keep the noise level down when you come

up to bed."

"Cecily, you're not going to stay up with me? I thought that after I finished eating we could, you know, make a few fireworks."

"There will be no fireworks here tonight." Cecily stomped up the stairs and got right back into bed.

CHAPTER 3

The visit to her primary care physician had led her down an unexpected road. After drawing her blood, he had determined that she was severely anemic and referred her to a hematologist. Cecily thought that this was an unnecessary step, but she was desperate to feel better. She could not imagine going another day dragging herself around like a sack of potatoes.

She'd had to wait another week for the appointment but finally, there she was filling out all the new patient paper work. They had no less than seventy-five questions on the forms. It was ridiculous and a little nerve-racking. Finally, she'd completed all of the forms, turned them in, paid her copay, and returned to her seat. Twenty minutes later she was called to the back.

"Hi, Mrs. Connors, what brings you in today?" The tall, thick nurse asked.

"I was referred by my primary doctor who seems to be very concerned about my anemia."

"Okay. May I ask you to step on the scale for me please?"

Cecily did as she was asked and was pleased to see that she was holding at a healthy one hundred thirty-five pounds. At one point when things started to disintegrate between she and Andrew, she'd packed on an extra fifteen pounds. Not healthy or attractive for her five-foot five inch frame. After catching a glimpse of herself in a store window one day, Cecily decided that she would not allow Andrew to steal her health and beauty the way he'd taken away so much of her joy.

"Please step this way and have a seat Mrs. Connors so that I can take your temperature and blood pressure."

"Of course." Cecily took a seat and opened her mouth to receive the thermometer. The nurse slipped the pressure cuff on Cecily's arm, pushed the button, and watched as the cuff tightened on her patients arm.

"Your temperature is normal and blood pressure is good. Please follow me."

A few steps and they were in the laboratory. "This is Mr. Everton; he'll draw your blood and then escort you to exam room two."

"Okay, thank you."

"How are you today?" The young man inquired.

"I'm okay, and you?"

"I'm fine, thank you." Cecily was so drained that she didn't notice the gentleman glancing at her from the corner of his eye. "Okay, there will be a small stick. Forgive me if I hurt you."

"I'll try and be brave," Cecily teased.

Two sticks later, Mr. Everton had his blood; Cecily had a couple of Band-Aids and was being escorted to exam room two.

"The doctor should be with you soon. Oh and sorry about having to stick you twice."

"No worries, Mr. Everton, I survived it," Cecily chuckled.

With a sheepish smile, he responded, "Please call me Carter."

"Alright then, Carter it is."

"Take care." Carter stepped back and closed the door as he made his exit.

Cecily pulled out her MP3 player and began to listen to a little music. She couldn't think of a better way to pass the time. It seemed that no one understood the role that music played in her life. No, she couldn't sing, couldn't carry a tune in a bucket, but music spoke to her soul. There was always a song that seemed to speak to whatever stage in life that she was in. Right now, Chrisette Michele was the artist that understood her most. Her song "Blame It On Me" expressed exactly how Cecily felt about her situation with Andrew. She didn't care what people thought, didn't care if she was held responsible for all the bad things in the marriage, she just wanted out. Cecily was so caught up in her music; she didn't realize that the doctor had entered the room. She felt a tap on her shoulder and her eyes flew open.

"Oh, Dr. Douglas, I'm sorry I didn't realize you'd come in."

"I didn't mean to startle you. That must be some good music."

"It is. Chrisette Michele is one of my favorites right now."

"I must agree that her *Epiphany* CD is really good. But, enough about music, what brings you in today?"

"Well let's see, I've been extremely tired lately. I have zero energy, it seems that a short walk across a parking lot causes me to have chest pains and leaves me totally out of breath. I've even started experiencing more joint pain than normal, and these headaches will not go away. My primary physician said that I'm very anemic and suggested I see you."

"Yes, according to the blood tests we just ran, you are certainly anemic. But I

have the lab running some additional tests that will hopefully shed a little more light on what's really going on with you. While we're waiting on the results, how about I ask you a few questions?"

"Sure, go right ahead." Cecily felt very comfortable with Dr. Douglas. She was a bit surprised because it normally took her a while to warm up to a new physician. More often than not, Cecily found doctors to be cold and stand-offish, but that was clearly not the case with Dr. Douglas. He was warm and inviting and Cecily immediately felt at ease with him. She'd just met him, but she completely trusted him with her health and well being.

"So tell me, Cecily, does anyone in your family have sickle cell anemia?"

"Actually, I do have a couple of cousins that have been long sufferers of sickle cell."

"Do you know if either of your parents carries the trait?"

"Oh wow, Dr. Douglas, they both do. And now that you have me thinking about this, my parents had a baby a few years before they had me. It was another little girl but she passed away in infancy. Apparently it was from the effects of sickle cell. I guess back then they really didn't know how to treat it."

Just as Dr. Douglas was about to speak, there was a knock at the door and one of the nurses stepped in. "Here are the other lab results you requested." She handed the paper to the doctor and stepped right back out, closing the door behind her.

Dr. Douglas looked over the lab results, looked up at Cecily with warm, caring eyes and began to speak. "Cecily, my suspicions have been confirmed, you have sickle cell anemia."

"But I don't understand, I thought that this was something that you were born with. How could I just develop a disease such as this?" Cecily's voice trembled as she spoke.

Dr. Douglas placed his hand on Cecily's hand in an effort to calm and comfort her. "You're correct; this is something that you were born with. A simple blood test would have revealed it years ago. It's amazing how some people don't begin to experience symptoms or have complications until they're older. Sometimes the burdens and stresses of life will cause it to reveal itself. You'd be surprised by the number of women that don't become symptomatic until they're a few months into their first pregnancy."

"This is just crazy. So what now, will I start to have uncontrollable pain? What will happen to me, Dr. Douglas?"

"Sickle cell can affect its patients in a variety of ways and yes, intense pain is generally associated with it. Right now though, my greatest concern is your low blood level. A big part in the treatment of sickle cell for many is blood transfusions. I strongly feel that that needs to be our first course of action. We can place you in the hospital for a couple of days. That will give us the opportunity to better evaluate your situation, get you transfused and alleviate your pain."

"Hospital! But I have kids I have to take care of and I don't want a transfusion. What about AIDS? People can get that from transfused blood, you know. Can't I just take some iron pills?" Cecily was almost hysterical.

"The blood is so closely screened that the threat of AIDS is virtually a non-issue. And you should not be taking iron pills at all. The anemia is not due to a lack of iron, but a blood disorder. More importantly, I think your children would rather be without you for a couple of days as opposed to a lifetime. You are now going to have to make your health the priority in your life."

CHAPTER 4

It had been two days since Cecily was admitted to the hospital and she was starting to get a little stir crazy. The good news was that her pain was now well controlled. The bad news, with all of the tests they were running she knew she'd be there for at least another two days. Cecily missed her babies and worried if they were being properly cared for. Her mom had been kind enough to watch after them while she was hospitalized and she was sure that Andrew was taking full advantage of the few days he had to himself. Funny thing is she hadn't seen Andrew since he'd dropped her off at the entrance to the hospital. He'd promised to come by and bring her some dinner. Lord knows the hospital food was awful. But not to Cecily's surprise, something came up with work and he wasn't able to make it. So she'd picked at her meal and decided to press the button on her medication pump. The liquid that ran through her IV alleviated her pain and helped her sleep through the long and lonely nights.

7:30a.m. and here they were to take her for a lung scan. Dr. Douglas was very thorough and wanted to be sure that her chest pain was not associated with a blood clot, something that was very common among sickle cell patients. Once she was returned to her room, Cecily was able to shower and get cleaned up for another day of needles and slow moving clocks. Her mind couldn't help but to drift to her home life and what she'd allowed herself to become. It was a sad situation and she was so tired of going along just to get along. She'd given up so much of herself, sacrificed what she wanted for the sake of providing a safe and secure home for her children. The more she thought about it, the more depressed she became, so she decided to turn on the television and tune into the soap operas, something she hadn't done in a long time. While her life seemed to be spinning out of control, it couldn't touch the drama of *The Young and The Restless.*

The knock at the door startled Cecily. She wasn't expecting anyone and the staff didn't bother knocking at all. "Come in," Cecily invited as she sat up a little straighter in the bed.

"Hey there, how are you today?" Carter asked as he glided into the room. Cecily looked at him and for a second found it difficult to speak.

"Hey, yourself. I'm fine, how are you?"

"I'm good. I hope you don't mind my stopping by?"

"Oh no, of course not," Cecily replied as she began to straighten her gown and self consciously run her hand over her hair. She knew she looked a mess, but she couldn't help but notice how good Carter looked. She took note of his six foot two inch slender frame. His smooth, milk chocolate complexion, soulful eyes and beautiful smile made it hard for her not to stare. Then she took notice of his baby face and thought, *Girl, snap out of it. You're married and he's young.*

Carter made his way over to the small couch and sat his satchel down. "Do you mind if I have a seat?"

"No, please make yourself comfortable. So tell me, Carter, what brings you to this neck of the woods?"

"Truthfully, I knew you were upset and nervous about all of this when you left the office the other day and I wanted to check on you. I wanted to make sure that all was going well. I hope that's okay?"

"That's very kind of you and I must say it's nice to see a somewhat familiar face. Now tell me, do you visit all of Dr. Douglas' patients in the hospital?"

Flashing that brilliant smile, Carter chuckled and replied, "Absolutely not." Then he reached into his satchel and pulled out a couple of DVD's. "I don't know if you're a big movie buff, but I thought I'd smuggle a couple in here, give you something to help pass the time."

"Wow. That was so nice of you. I really appreciate it." The grin on Cecily's face was as wide as a dollar bill.

"I didn't know what type of movies you like so I grabbed a comedy and a drama. I hope that you'll find them entertaining."

"I know that I will, Carter. I've found that it gets a little lonely in here at night so these will make perfect company."

Pointing to the television, Carter asked, "So you enjoy that stuff?"

"What can I say; I got hooked on the soap operas a long time ago. Besides, there isn't anything else on worth watching. But I must say that I find this story line a little hard to believe. That guy is her husband, but look at how much younger he is than her. A little unrealistic, don't you think?"

"Not at all. Look at her, if the woman looks good and is maintaining herself, I don't see the problem."

"Oh, I see." Before Cecily could form another sentence, Carter's cell phone rang. It was the office letting him know that he was needed.

"I'm sorry I have to run off."

"No apologies necessary. Thank you for coming by and bringing the movies, that was very thoughtful. I really appreciate it."

"You're more than welcome. Before I leave, I'm going to write my number up here on the board, just in case you want to talk or need anything." Carter took the marker and proceeded to write his name and number on the lower corner of the dry erase board. "Oh, I just thought of something. I typically don't answer unknown numbers. Care to share yours?"

Cecily couldn't help but smile at the slick way he was trying to obtain her information and she was unable to resist. "Sure, why not. My cell is 404-555-3555."

"Got it, please feel free to call anytime, Cecily." Carter flashed her one last smile then turned and made his exit.

CHAPTER 5

Two days had passed since Cecily was released from the hospital. Rhonda, her nearest and dearest friend of fifteen years, was kind enough to pick her up from the hospital. Her dearly beloved husband was unable to pull himself away from work long enough to give her a ride home. Or at least that's what he told her, but she was sure she knew the real reason. Andrew's secretary had let Cecily in on the rumors that were flying around about him and the hot new associate attorney. The sad part was that Cecily couldn't care less. If being with the office tart meant that Andrew would leave her alone then their affair was fine with her.

Saturday morning usually meant preparing pancakes for the kids and giving the house a thorough cleaning before heading out for the afternoon. But her mom hadn't returned the children to her yet. Mom thought it best that Cecily have an extra couple of days to rest up and for all of the narcotics to get out of her system. Cecily appreciated all that her mother did for her, but she was ready to have her babies back. She had eaten a late breakfast, thanks to Andrew, who had run out and picked up a little something from a fast food joint. Once she'd finished that, she moved about the house cleaning up the mess that had been created in her absence. Cecily was hanging up clothes when her cell phone rang. She couldn't help but smile when she saw that it was Carter.

"Hello."

"Hi there, this is Carter. Did I catch you at a bad time?"

"Oh no, just taking care of a little house work. How are you?"

"I'm fine. I wanted to call and check on you, make sure you were feeling better."

"I am. Thank you. I'm feeling much better. Seems that I have a little extra pep in my step and I like it."

With a chuckle Carter replied, "That's really good to hear. So what are your big plans for the day?"

"Nothing too exciting. I'm having dinner with the girls and then back home to enjoy the quiet before my children return home tomorrow."

"I see. So how many children do you have?"

"Two, a girl and a boy and I'm so blessed to have them. I think that they are the only reason I maintain my sanity. Do you have any children?"

"No, not yet. I'd like to though…someday."

"Well who knows, that special person could be just around the corner, ready, willing and able to make you a proud papa."

"Wow, let's not get too far ahead of ourselves."

There was a slight pause before Carter spoke again. "So tell me Cecily, what's your story?"

"Married with children and living your typical life in the suburbs."

"Is that a happy life?"

"Like everything else, it has its moments. Now it's my turn to ask a question. Why aren't you spending your Saturday talking to some hot little thing and making plans for the evening?"

"I thought I *was* talking to a hot little thing."

Cecily was grateful that he couldn't see the grin that spread across her face. She

was well aware that he probably had his fair share of women and that he was just running game. But the attention was still nice. It had been a long time since she had even entertained this type of conversation from a man other than Andrew. She and Carter's conversation went on for a few minutes more.

"Well, it's been nice talking with you, Carter. I have an appointment with Dr. Douglas next week and I'll make sure to return your movies to you."

"Maybe you can return them to me over lunch after your appointment?"

"Maybe, let's just play it by ear, okay?"

"Okay, that's fair enough. Enjoy the rest of your day, Cecily. Goodbye."

"Bye-bye, Carter."

ððð

Marshall's was a little neighborhood sports bar that served pretty decent edibles. Rhonda suggested it for the girl's night out because the atmosphere was so festive and the music was always good. The three girlfriends were seated at a high top table in the center of the establishment. Within a couple of minutes, a waitress approached the table and took their drink orders. They continued to peruse the menu until the woman returned with two small glasses of vodka and cranberry juice and Cecily's Shirley Temple. They placed their food orders and then let the conversation flow.

"So has Andrew been waiting on you hand and foot since everything with your health and the hospital stay happened?" Karen quizzed.

Before Cecily could respond, Rhonda blurted out "Child please, that busta wouldn't even pick her up from the hospital."

"You are kidding me?"

"No she's not." Cecily hung her head a little as she continued to speak. "I understand that he has to work, but I thought he'd be able to tear himself away long enough to drive me home. I don't know why I thought that, seeing as how he dropped me off when I had to check in."

Karen was shocked. "You mean he didn't stay with you? Didn't make sure that you were all settled in?"

"It's no biggie," Cecily lied. "Things have been so screwed up between us that nothing he does, or doesn't do, should surprise me."

"That's some bullshit," Rhonda snarled. "He vowed to love you through sickness and health, rich or poor, and all the other foolishness they include with it. Yet he hasn't managed to be there for much of anything when it comes to your needs or desires." Rhonda took a sip of her drink and rolled her eyes as a way of expressing her disgust with Andrew and his selfish behavior. Rhonda had always been a no-nonsense kind of girl that shot straight from the hip. She was very selective about whom she let share her life and her space and if you were among the ones privileged enough to be called her friend, then you knew that you had a real treasure. For a true friend, Rhonda would lay her life on the line. "That's the very reason that I don't ever see myself getting married. Once they get married, men become selfish little boys who think that the world should revolve around them and them alone. I refuse to live with that kind of behavior."

"That is not a fair statement, Rhonda. You should be really careful about painting an entire gender with such a broad brush." Karen chimed in. Karen was known to be the defender of anyone perceived as the underdog and for her; any man viewed in a negative light was the underdog. She was a really smart woman when it came to business, but lacked all common sense when it came to relationships. Karen would become a doormat for almost any tall, dark, handsome man that showed her a bit of interest. Her ultimate dream was to be married with children and she couldn't understand why Cecily complained about her husband. She thought that Cecily should just be happy that she had a man.

"Ladies, can we please enjoy tonight and not discuss Andrew anymore?" Cecily pleaded. "I'll have to return home to his foolishness soon enough so let me enjoy this time without thinking about him."

"Fine with me," Karen retorted. "But I still don't understand how you can be so bothered by a man that gets up and goes to work every day, pays all the bills, and takes care of his kids. What do you want from the man, blood?"

"Karen, shut the hell up!" Rhonda demanded. "If you knew what to do with a man and how to handle a marriage, you wouldn't be divorced. He never would have left your ass. So why don't you back off a little and let Cecily, hell, let all of us enjoy the rest of the evening?"

"Whatever, Rhonda. We won't talk about Cecily and Andrew anymore. But let me tell you, if you talk to me like that again, I'm going to smack you."

Cecily and Rhonda looked at one another and burst out laughing. They both knew that Karen didn't have the balls to smack a gnat. Karen began to laugh at herself after a moment. She was surprised that the threat of violence even escaped her mouth. The remainder of the night was filled with food, fun, dancing, and laughter. It was exactly what Cecily needed to distract her from the issues of her home life.

CHAPTER 6

Cecily got up Sunday morning and began to prepare for church. She fixed the kids a light breakfast and laid their clothes out for them while they ate. It wasn't long before the entire family was walking out the door with the anticipation of enjoying a spirit filled service.

As usual, the Pastor brought a mighty word, one that would serve as spiritual food and inspiration for the week to come. After the benediction, Cecily held the kids hands and began to leave the sanctuary, assuming that Andrew was right behind her. Needless to say, she was mistaken. Cecily stood in the lobby and watched as Andrew hugged and shamelessly flirted with his so called friend. This woman was allegedly the ex-girlfriend of Andrew's college roommate. She was a fair skinned, busty woman that, without fail, sat in close proximity to Andrew. Of course, he denied that she did that on purpose, but out of a congregation of twelve hundred people, Cecily found it hard to believe that the seating arrangement was always a coincidence. Ten minutes later Andrew finally emerged from the sanctuary, followed by his *friend*, who made a point of looking at Cecily with a sinister grin plastered across her face.

The ride to Houston's, their favorite restaurant, was a quiet one. The only noise was that of giggles and low chatter made by the children in the back seat. "What's wrong with you?" Andrew asked as he glanced at Cecily out the corner of his eye.

"I think you already know the answer to that, Andrew."

"What, am I psychic now?"

"Every Sunday it's the same thing. You disrespect me with that hooch and then

pretend that you have no idea what the matter could be."

"Why does she have to be a hooch and what is wrong with me speaking with a friend? We're in church for goodness sake, what do you think is going to happen? Think I'm going to jump her bones on one of the pews?"

"I wouldn't put it past you and don't you dare defend her to me. I'll call that hooch, that whore, that slut anything that I want to." Cecily spat back in a venomous whisper.

"I'm so sick of your paranoia, Cecily. I am not trying to bed every woman that I speak to. Sometimes I'm just being sociable."

"*Sometimes*! Did you really just say *sometimes*? So all the other times that you speak to women you really are trying to bed them. Unbelievable."

"You know that's not what I meant, baby. I was only trying to say that I have female friends, but I have no romantic interest in any of them."

"Go to hell, Andrew," Cecily responded as they pulled into a space in front of the restaurant.

The family had enjoyed their meal in virtual silence. Once home, everyone changed out of their church clothes. Cecily and the kids put on comfortable lounging clothing. Andrew, however, had changed into his favorite True Religion jeans and button down shirt.

"Where are you going?" Cecily inquired.

"I'm meeting one of the guys for a drink. Is that a problem?"

"Wow, so much for quality time. Being here with your family is something you have no interest in anymore, huh?"

"Cecily, we can't even go to church without it being an argument. The kids don't give a crap if I step out for a bit. And I don't get why you care. It's not like if I stay here we are going to make mad, passionate love or anything."

"Maybe if you weren't the most selfish lover to walk the Earth, we would. Maybe if you cared as much for my satisfaction as you do your own, we would. Maybe if I meant more to you than just a warm place to put it, we would. But since none of that applies, you're right; I don't care about your leaving. Bye!"

"Bitch."

"Your mama."

Andrew looked at Cecily as if he could choke the life out of her and the look she returned dared him to come near her. Instead, he grabbed his keys and stormed out of the room. Cecily dropped to the bed and wept. This was not the way that their love and marriage was supposed to go. She had no desire for her children to be the products of divorce, but she couldn't imagine spending the rest of her life like this.

ððð

Friday had rolled around so quickly and Cecily found herself having to scramble and gather her things so that she could rush off to her appointment with Dr. Douglas. Fortunately, the mid day traffic wasn't too heavy and before she knew it, she was whipping her car into a parking space outside of the doctor's office. She reached over and placed Carter's DVD's into her oversized hand bag and hastily made her way to the professional building.

This was such a busy practice that Cecily had mentally prepared herself for a long wait. To her pleasant surprise, there was only one other person waiting to be seen. She signed in and took a seat. Within ten minutes, she was summoned to the back where her vitals were taken and she was escorted to the lab for a blood draw.

"Hello, Cecily. Please have a seat."

"Hi, Carter, how are you today?" Cecily cooed as she slid into the seat that was offered.

"Much better now," he stated with a sly grin. "I hate to stick you, but I have to. Forgive me in advance for any discomfort that this may cause."

"No worries, I'm sure it won't be so bad."

Carter carefully but tightly placed the tourniquet around Cecily's arm. Once he located a viable vein, he rubbed the area with alcohol and as gently as he could, inserted the butterfly needle into her arm. A slight flinch let him know that despite his efforts, Cecily still felt the pinch of the needle. After filling two tubes with her blood, he removed the needle and bandaged her arm.

"I hope I didn't hurt you too badly?"

"No, not at all, you were fine. Oh, by the way, I have your DVD's." Cecily reached for her bag and began to remove the movies.

"Does this mean that you won't be able to return them over lunch?"

"Yes, it does. I would actually enjoy having lunch with you, but school lets out early today and I have to get back to my side of town to get my children."

The disappointment on Carters face was unmistakable. "I understand. Family first."

"I'm sorry, but hey, maybe another time?"

"You know, you could come over. We could grab a little something to eat and maybe watch a movie."

Not understanding what came over her and possessed her to accept, Cecily heard herself saying, "sure, why not?"

ððð

Cecily had returned home from her Saturday outing with the kids only to find the babysitter waiting at the house. She'd asked the young lady why was she there, but the girl only said that Mr. Connors had called her over. Not sure of what was going on, Cecily skeptically made her way upstairs where she found Andrew taking a shower.

"Why is Candace here?" Cecily asked suspiciously.

"Well hello to you too."

Sarcastically Cecily replied, "Hello, dear, how are you?"

"Ah, now that's better. I'm fine, sweetie. How are you today?"

"I'm fine, Andrew. Now what is Candace doing here?"

Andrew stepped out of the shower and gently kissed his wife on the cheek. "We've been arguing so much lately that I thought maybe a night out would do us both some good. Seems like even the kids are on edge around here. An evening of good music, good food, and conversation might get us back in sync which will in turn have a positive effect on the kids. It's a win, win for us all."

"Wow, I must say that this is a pleasant surprise. Where are we heading? I want to dress appropriately for the location."

"There's a live band playing at Kat's that's supposed to be really good, but first I figured we'd grab dinner at Blue Plate. That sound alright with you?"

"That sounds great. Let me jump in the shower real quick and I'll be ready before you know it."

An hour later the normally argumentative couple was sharing a bottle of wine and lively conversation in the upscale restaurant. The food arrived at the table and it was better than either of them had imagined it would be. Cecily sat smiling at her husband while trying to remember the last time they had enjoyed one another this much. The memory was so far gone that she could no longer recall it, so she decided to just live in the moment.

It had been a long time since Andrew had shown any interest in her career. To say that Cecily was glad to have him asking about her job would be an understatement. She went on and on about the office politics, the promotion that she was up for, and the new direction she hoped her career would be taking. Andrew listened intently and actually felt a sense of pride over his wife's accomplishments. He also realized that he hadn't been as encouraging with her career as he should've been and made a mental note to do better.

Kat's, a small lounge known for their music and Martini's, did not disappoint. The featured band was amazing! The lead singer's sultry voice was intoxicating. She was very reminiscent of Anita Baker; one of Cecily's all time favorite artists. The happy couple sat there holding hands and swaying to the music when someone approached their table.

"Well, look at you two looking all in love and stuff."

Cecily turned around to see Karen and another young lady standing at their table. "Hey, Karen, what are you doing here?" She asked with a bit of surprise.

"I'm out celebrating with my new roommate, Hannah. As you know, this economy has hit me hard, but now that I have someone to share the bills with, things are bound to get better."

"That's great and it's so nice to meet you Hannah." Cecily said with an extended hand. "Oh and this is my husband, Andrew."

Andrew turned to face the woman he was being introduced to and the surprised look on his face was undeniable. Hannah looked just as surprised as she shook Andrew's hand and tried to step back and blend in with the rest of the folks standing around. Cecily looked at Karen as if she were asking, *did you see that*? Karen on the other hand was behaving as if she'd noticed nothing unusual. She exchanged a couple more pleasantries and excused herself so that Cecily and Andrew could resume their date.

The ride home was a little quiet as Cecily sat contemplating as to whether she should ask about the awkward introduction between Hannah and Andrew. The night had been so pleasant and she wanted it to continue, but Cecily couldn't stop herself from asking the question that had been nagging her since they were in Kat's.

"Babe, it seemed as if you were surprised to see Karen's new roommate, Hannah. Both of you were a little taken aback, had you two met before?"

"No, I've never seen her before. I guess I was a little surprised that Karen had taken a roommate. I knew that things had been financially tight for her, but I didn't know that they were that bad."

"Yes, after the divorce Karen was left with little to nothing. That ex-husband of hers really raked her over the coals, so this roommate situation is a real blessing for her. But just to be sure, you've never met Hannah before."

"Not at all, babe and if she were to walk up to me tomorrow I probably wouldn't even recognize her."

Cecily decided to take her husband at his word and focus on enjoying the rest of their evening. They arrived home, paid the babysitter, and spent the remainder of the night making love and sleeping in each other's arms.

CHAPTER 7

It had been a long day at work and Cecily was glad that her mom had called and asked if it were okay for her to pick the kids up from school and take them home with her. Her mom found great enjoyment in spending time with her grandchildren. It wasn't unusual for her to pick them up, help with homework, and take them to dinner at their favorite neighborhood restaurant. And of course, this was quite a treat for Rachel and Brian. Shortly after hanging up with her mom, Cecily's line rang again.

"Cecily Connors, how may I help you?"

"Girl, I know you saw my number on that caller I.D., stop playing like you're a professional," Rhonda teased.

"I am a professional." Cecily declared with laughter in her voice. "Now can I help you with something or did you call just to harass me?"

"I want you to meet me at Twist after work. It's been a hell of a day and I could use a drink."

"Count me in, but I can't stay long. I have to get home before my mom arrives to drop the kids off. Did you call and invite Karen?"

"No, am I supposed to invite her to everything that we do?"

"Not necessarily, but I want her to come because I want to ask her about her knew roommate and how she knows Andrew."

"What new roommate and how do you know she knows Andrew?"

"Look, just call Karen, tell her to arrive thirty minutes after our meeting time so that I can catch you up before she gets there."

"No problem, consider it done."

By five-thirty Cecily was walking through the doors at Twist. Rhonda was already belly up to the bar sipping on a glass of wine.

"Couldn't wait for a sistah?"

"Girl sit down and start talking. Your glass is on the way." Rhonda nodded at the bartender who immediately poured Cecily a glass of Moscato and sat it before her.

Cecily recounted the events of her date night with Andrew as well as his denial of having ever met Hannah. She described how it was clearly an uncomfortable moment for both of them as well as how Karen didn't seem to pick up on any of what was going on.

"Did you ask Karen if she knew of a previous meeting or encounter between Andrew and this Hannah chick?"

"No, I haven't really had a chance. That's why I wanted her to meet us today. And speak of the devil; she's walking through the door right now with Hannah in tow."

Rhonda gave Hannah the once over, checked her out head to toe. She took notice of her compact but very shapely body, her milky complexion, pretty facial features, and shoulder length blond hair. No denying she was an attractive woman, but her looks would not give her a free pass when came to messing with a married man. Especially Rhonda's best friend's man.

"Hey diva's." Karen squealed as she wrapped her arms around her friends one at a time. Karen always made such a production when the three of them got together. She was especially excited today because she was hoping that Cecily and Rhonda would take the time to get to know Hannah and welcome her into their little circle of friends.

"Hi ladies. Nice to see you again, Hannah." Cecily spoke with the sweetest voice. She learned a long time ago that you can catch more flies with sugar than with vinegar. She wanted both women to feel comfortable with her, especially Hannah.

"It's good to see you again as well, Cecily. I hope you don't mind that I decided to tag along?"

"Not at all, any friend of Karen is a friend of ours. Isn't that right, Rhonda?"

"Humph…if you say so."

Cecily nudged Rhonda in an attempt to make her change her attitude, or at least fake it.

"I mean of course." Rhonda chimed with a broad smile, her poor attempt to seem warm and sincere.

Continuing with her forced grin, Rhonda politely offered the women a seat at the bar. Cecily smiled her thanks and approval.

"So Hannah, tell us a little about yourself. You know, where you're from, what you do, who you're dating, and all that good stuff?" Rhonda quizzed as she took another sip of her wine.

With all eyes on her, Hannah took a deep breath and decided to just start talking and be as honest as possible. After all, these could potentially be the best friends she'd have here in Georgia. "Well, I'm originally from Kansas City. I am a hair stylist by trade but I'm currently studying to be a nurse. I've met a couple of folks since moving here but not anyone I'm really interested in dating. It seems that all the good ones are already married or sadly, they're gay. So that doesn't leave me a lot of options."

"That sounds typical, the good ones being already hitched that is." Cecily was trying to speak in a manner that was light and carefree. "Do you mind if I ask if you've ever had any involvement with a married man?"

Karen was shocked by Cecily's question and was wondering where she was trying to go with this conversation. Her sudden uncomfortable demeanor did not go unnoticed by Rhonda. Karen was known to switch in her seat and fidget when she was nervous and at this point, she was damn near dancing on the bar stool.

Karen wasn't the only one that was suddenly struck by a case of nerves, Hannah was right there with her. The girl began to stutter and sputter like a 1979 Pinto. "I---I once had an---an affair with a ma---ma---married man, but that was a---a long time ago. I vowed to never do---do---do that again."

Rhonda and Cecily looked at one another as if to say 'what the hell!' There was obviously something going on but Cecily wasn't sure that continuing to push the subject today was the best way to proceed. She looked at Rhonda and gave her the hand gesture across the neck and Rhonda knew to shut that line of questioning down. But Rhonda always had an alternate plan.

"Alright, enough questions, I came here to relax and blow off a little steam. Bartender, drinks for everyone." Rhonda requested. Immediately you could see the relief ease across the faces of Karen and Hannah. Rhonda also ordered appetizers and continued to let the liquor flow. The four of them laughed, talked and drank for another hour. Karen and Hannah threw back drink after drink and didn't seem to notice that Cecily and Rhonda had been nursing the same drinks almost the entire time. It used to be only on special occasions that Karen would drink, but since the divorce, Patron had become one of her closest friends.

"Well ladies, as much as I hate to leave this little party, I've got to go and get my babies." Cecily had everyone's attention except Hannah's. Waving her hand in front of Hannah's face, Cecily quizzed, "Girl did you hear me?"

"Oh yeah, be careful going home. It was good seeing you again." Hannah responded without ever turning her head away from the man that had her so captivated. Cecily followed her gaze and discovered that Hannah was lost in a tall, well built man with the perfect smile and dark chocolate complexion that stood across the room. A closer look revealed that the dude looked eerily like Cecily's husband.

"So, that's your type?"

"Absolutely." Hannah responded as she licked her lips as if she were staring at the last pork chop on the buffet table.

"You know, he reminds me of my husband."

Hannah, now speaking a little more freely, immediately shot back, "Huh… you're right. As a matter of fact, when I first met Andrew I thought 'damn his wife is lucky.' Better watch him girl, don't let someone else come and snatch him."

Without thinking, Cecily lunged towards Hannah. "What do you mean the first time you met Andrew? How the hell do you know my husband?" Rhonda tried to put some space between her best friend and what was looking like her new enemy. Karen on the other hand sobered up long enough to realize that this situation was only going to get worse. With that in mind, she snatched Hannah's drink from her hand and ushered her out of the establishment.

Karen dragged Hannah behind her like a little rag doll. "Get your ass in the car!" Karen demanded. They buckled up and Karen tore out of the parking lot as if she were running for her life. "What was that, Hannah? I told you to watch what you say around them. You weren't supposed to give Cecily any indication that you'd ever met Andrew, and instead you sang like a damn canary. Now she knows that there is some kind of connection."

"I'm sorry, Karen, I asked you not to put me in this situation in the first place. I specifically said that I had no desire to meet your friends, let alone hang out with them."

"Don't you realize how suspicious it would look for me to have a new roommate and not ever introduce her to the people closest to me? You realize that you all would have eventually met; they do come and visit me every now and then. Gosh…you have to stop being so damn stupid."

"Call me stupid one more time and I promise it will be your last. Don't forget, I'm doing all of this to help you out."

Karen's normally meek demeanor had been replaced by some she-devil. "Helping me, are you serious? If it weren't for me your ass would be in jail. Don't forget, I'm the parole officer that made it possible for you to roam the streets a free woman. I put my job, my livelihood on the line for you. So unless you want to find yourself sharing a cell with Big Bertha, you will watch your mouth around my friends and follow through with your end of the bargain."

Hannah held on to the door handle in an attempt to keep from being flung from the car. Karen was driving like a lunatic and Hannah knew that she would follow through with her threats. Tears began to burn her eyes as she thought about what she would ultimately have to do. Taking another life was not something Hannah imagined she'd ever have to do again

CHAPTER 8

The kids were sleeping and Cecily was lying in bed channel surfing. She had been waiting hours for Andrew to come home. Initially she was furious and paced the floor in an effort to calm down. Soon she discovered that an hour of continuous walking was exhausting, even if it was just around her kitchen island. Cecily's eyelids were heavy and she was about to give in to sleep when she heard the garage door going up.

"What are you still doing up, honey?"

"I'm waiting for my loving, faithful husband to come home to me. I didn't realize that it would take so long. Where have you been?"

"The office, I had a ton of work to do. Now, why don't you go ahead and tell me what I've done *this* time, Cecily so that we can get this argument over with."

"Do I look like a fool to you? It's two in the morning and your office building is locked up tight as a drum at 10:00p.m. every single night."

"Damn, I went out with a co-worker for drinks after we left work. Why the hell are you hounding me? I'm tired and don't feel like all this shit tonight."

"You know…maybe I am a fool, Andrew. I know we've had more than our fair share of problems, but after our date night I actually thought that things were changing for the better. You made love to me like you actually wanted me. For the first time in a long time you put me first, you weren't selfish."

Andrew stepped out of his pants and into a pair of pajama bottoms. "Good night, Cecily." He climbed into bed and turned his back to his crying wife. In a last ditch effort to mend their marriage, Cecily gently reached her hand out to stroke her husband's back and that's when she noticed the open scratches. Without saying a word, she eased out of bed, retrieved a bottle of alcohol and doused it on Andrew's back. Surprisingly, his screams didn't wake the kids.

"What the hell is wrong with you bitch, have you lost your damn mind?"

"I didn't want the scratches that your whore, Hannah left on your back to get infected you sorry bastard."

"How many times do I have to tell you that I don't even know that girl? She ain't even my type." The scowl on Andrews face was one of pure rage. At the moment, strangling his wife would have brought him more joy than anything else he could imagine.

"I spoke with her this evening and Hannah admitted that you two knew one another. She even went so far as to tell me to watch my back so that someone else doesn't come in and swoop you up. Now do you want to rethink this whole lie about you not knowing her?"

"The only thing I want to rethink is staying in this sorry ass marriage!"

ððð

It had been two months since the alcohol incident, but Andrew, despite all of his threats to leave, hadn't said another word about abandoning their marriage. Cecily had come to the conclusion that he simply didn't want to deal with the issue of child support. But enough of that, she wanted to put Andrew and their problems out of her mind, for a while anyway.

Cecily walked through the door of Dr. Douglas' office, signed in and greeted the receptionist. It was time for her follow up visit and she hoped that her blood work would show that another transfusion would not be required for a very long time. As usual, the nurse ushered her to the back, took her vital signs and escorted her to the lab. Carter turned to face his next patient and instantly, a smile crept across both their faces.

"Well hello Mrs. Connors, how are you?"

With a child-like demeanor, Cecily replied, "I'm just peachy, Mr. Everton how are you today?"

"I'm disappointed." Carter dropped his head and begun to move around the room retrieving all of the necessary supplies to obtain her blood sample.

"May I ask why you're so disappointed?"

"I was expecting company a few weeks back but the lady never showed. I was so hurt."

"I'm sorry, Carter. I knew that it would be inappropriate and I didn't want to send the wrong message."

"I figured as much, but it was my intention that we would just enjoy a movie and share conversation. Believe me; I would never want to put you in an uncomfortable situation."

"Well, seeing as how I still haven't seen the movies you selected for me, I guess I can swing by your place and watch one of them. You'll have to let me know when it'll be a good day and time for you and I promise to show up, with popcorn."

"This Friday works for me, shall we say around seven?"

Cecily was caught off guard, she didn't expect for him to suggest a time so soon. She blinked a couple of times but didn't allow herself time to fully digest what she was about to do. "Umm…sure, Friday works for me."

"Great!" Carter exclaimed with the excitement of a kid in a candy store. "Here is my address." He said as he scribbled it on the back of a business card. I'll expect you at seven."

Cecily left her appointment satisfied with her test results but unsure of her decision to see Carter outside of the doctor's office. She had never entertained the possibility of starting a new friendship with someone of the male persuasion since vowing to love, honor, and cherish Andrew. Cecily could still vividly recall standing in front of a church packed with family and friends. She thought that that would forever be the happiest day of her life. Sadly, that happiness had been replaced by feelings of regret and a longing for freedom. Andrew had shown time and time again that he was not the man she thought he was, didn't have the strength she thought he had and faithfulness meant absolutely nothing to him. Still, Cecily knew that her husband's betrayal was not a permission slip for her start behaving as if she were a single woman.

Friday seemed to have come so quickly. Cecily hadn't been able to concentrate on anything other than her pending movie night with Carter. She had reached for the phone and threatened to cancel at least six times, but something was pushing her to go. Thankfully, her mother had already made arrangements to keep the kids for the weekend. Since her father's death, Brian and Rachel were the ones that filled the void in her mother's life.

After work Cecily went straight home and began to prepare for her evening. She packed the kids weekend bags and had them waiting at the door for her mother. She'd braided Rachel's hair so that her mom wouldn't have to bother with combing it for the next couple of days and they had just returned from getting Brian a haircut. Shortly after their return, her mother rang the doorbell.

"Hey baby, how are you today?" Mom asked as she pulled Cecily into a warm hug.

"I'm fine Mom, how are you? More importantly, are you sure you want the kids for the entire weekend?"

"It's just two days, Cecily. Besides, we have a good time together. They are well behaved, I can take them anywhere without fear of them cutting the fool on me.

Trust me, if they were little demon seeds, I wouldn't be bothered for a minute."

"Well I know that they are looking forward to spending time with Grandma. They said something about Billy Bob's?"

"Oh yes, that's a little place we discovered in Conyers. They have video games, roller skating and pizza, but without the extreme crowds of Chuck E. Cheese's. You know I can't stand that Chuck E. Cheese, all those loud, unruly kids."

"Yes, I know, I can't stand that overcrowded place either. Too much going on for me. Mom, you know I appreciate the time you spend with my kids, they adore you and I'm so thankful for you all's relationship."

"Now you know those are my buddies, my road dogs. Besides, I enjoy them way more than I do that Abigail, always got her nose in a dream book trying to figure out the lottery number. That mess gets on my nerves. And if she asks me about my dreams one more time I'm going to scream."

Cecily was bent over in laughter. "You know you love Abigail, y'all have been friends for years. Who knows, one of these days you might share your dream and the number for it will hit. You could both be rich."

"As much as she loves money! Humph, she'd never tell me the right number for fear that she might have to split the winnings with me. But enough about her, where are my babies? We have got to get a move on."

Cecily went to the back room, told the kids that Grandma was waiting for them and they took off running to the front door. After plenty of hugs and kisses they were gone. Cecily knew that she would miss them but was thankful that the plans were already set so that she wouldn't have to lie to anyone about why she needed a babysitter. Andrew had already made it clear that he wouldn't be in until late, so he was very much a non-issue.

The hot water from the shower felt like heaven as it flowed over Cecily's body. She washed away the stresses of the day and allowed the warmth of the water and scent of her body wash to calm her nerves. As usual, she lotioned every inch of her body and covered herself with a fine mist of Cashmere. She'd already chosen a nice pair of jeans, blouse and heels to wear. Cecily spent far more time picking out her undergarments. While she had no intentions of allowing them to be seen, her panties and bras had a huge effect on how she felt about herself. She had an amazing lingerie collection that allowed her to always feel her feminine best. Finally, she settled on a black, lace thong with matching bra. Not the type of underwear she wore everyday but she figured *why not*?

It was 7:15 and Cecily was pulling into the driveway of 559 Lincoln Court. It was a very nice, quiet townhome community. She parked her car, took a few deep breaths, and jumped out of the driver's side door before she changed her mind and went back home. She knocked twice and the door was opened. There stood Carter in all of his handsome glory inviting her in. Cecily nervously crossed the threshold and Carter closed the door behind her.

"It's good to see you. Please come on in and make yourself comfortable. Did you have any trouble finding me?"

"No, I came straight here which is surprising considering how much I depend on my navigation system," Cecily responded with a nervous giggle.

"Well, as you can see I'm not properly dressed. Please have a seat, make yourself at home. I'm going to jump into the shower real quick. I promise I won't be long. Oh, can I get you something to drink before I dash off?"

"No thank you, I'm fine."

"You sure?"

"I'm positive. I'll be waiting right here when you're all done." Cecily settled into the sofa while Carter ran off to the shower. Cecily thought it was pretty odd that he'd keep her waiting while he showered. She'd expected him to be dressed, looking all clean and dapper. But on the other hand, this extra time gave her a chance to calm her nerves. While she sat and waited, she noticed a couple of photo albums and hoped he wouldn't mind her thumbing through them. As she flipped page after page and looked around at the photos on his walls and end tables, one thing became very apparent to her, family was of the utmost importance to Carter. Fifteen minutes later she was still flipping pages and hadn't noticed him watching her from around the corner. He eased on into the room and sat beside her, as she turned the pages of his life he explained who the people were that surrounded him in each picture.

"Enough of this, are you hungry?"

"I guess I could eat, what did you have in mind?"

"There's a great little Mexican place not too far from here. Does that sound appealing to you?"

"Mexican sounds great." Cecily grabbed her handbag and stood to her feet. Carter stood up as well and Cecily couldn't help but notice the height difference, she loved how he towered over her, it made her feel protected. And he was of course a perfect gentleman, opening and closing doors for her along the way. They decided to get their food from Qdoba to go. It didn't take long before they were back at Carter's place enjoying their meal and good conversation.

"I can't eat another bite." Cecily proclaimed.

"I'm pretty full myself. Are you comfortable with retiring to my bedroom to watch a movie? Sorry but that just happens to be where the only television in the house is located."

Cecily noticed that there was no television in the living room while she sat and waited for Carter. The only entertainment in that area of the house was his stereo system that piped beautiful music throughout the house. But she couldn't miss his extensive movie collection. She contemplated how comfortable or uncomfortable she might be with this situation, but then figured *what the hell.* "I suppose that will be fine."

Carter led the way to his room and insisted that Cecily make herself comfortable while he placed their movie selection into the DVD player. When he finished, he turned around to join her on the bed and couldn't help but giggle a little when he found that she was sitting as proper as she possibly could on the edge of the bed with her legs crossed.

"You're going to sit like that and watch the entire movie? Please, kick off your shoes and make yourself at home."

Cecily took notice of her posture and had to laugh at herself, she was indeed stiff as a board. So she kicked off her heels, crawled up on the king sized bed and relaxed into a much more comfortable position. Before she realized it, she was enjoying the movie and using Carter as her own personal pillow.

"Are you okay…comfortable? Would you like a pillow?" Carter quizzed as he gently stroked her hair.

"Oh, am I making you uncomfortable, am I too heavy?

"No, of course not. You're fine. I just want to make sure you're all good."

Slightly turning her head to face Carter, Cecily responded with a warm smile, "I actually like the pillow that I have."

Their gaze lingered for several seconds, long enough for Carter to draw her in for a kiss. A gentle, sweet kiss that melted the remainder of the mile high wall of protection that Cecily thought she'd built up. This wall was to defend her from lustful feelings and it was failing her miserably. One gentle kiss led to another and another until the kisses became deeper and deeper causing an insurmountable amount of passion to rise within the two of them. Carter had repositioned himself above Cecily as he continued to kiss and caress her. How could it be possible that his touch was both strong and gentle? He touched her in a way that said 'I want you' and that was something that Cecily had not felt for a very long time. And as her clothes were being peeled from her body, she could hear her guardian angel screaming for her to stop. But the lust that filled her seemed to have glued her mouth shut only allowing soft moans to escape. Before the full realization of what was happening hit her, Carter was lingering above her putting on a condom and still, no objections tumbled from her lips. Carter lowered himself, began to kiss Cecily once again as he gently entered her warmth. He took her breath away. They stroked and moved in one position and then another, ultimately landing Cecily on top. And though she had been married for years, this was the first time that any man had touched her or moved her to an overflowing orgasm. Her river spilled freely over Carter causing him to come stronger and harder than he ever had before. They collapsed into each other's arms and he held her as if it were something he did every day. Neither of them wanted the night to end, but Cecily knew that she had to be on her way.

The ride home was like no other. Cecily's mind was flying. She couldn't believe what she had done. She never imagined that she would cheat; it simply wasn't who she was or what she did. Or so she thought. Her mind flashed back to Carter and what they'd just done, and then flashes of Andrew invaded her mind and she waited. She waited for the feelings of guilt to ravage her but they didn't. She could only rationalize that the guilt would eventually come after she came down from the cloud she was still floating on.

CHAPTER 9

It was a bit of a shock for Cecily to find Andrew at home. Though she didn't get in until 2:30am, she still hadn't expected him to be cuddled up in bed sleeping. She'd tiptoed to the bathroom, gently closed the door and eased into a hot shower. She stood still as a million beads of water pulsated over her flesh. Her mind, once again, flashed back to Carter and the things that they'd done. She forced herself to shake the thoughts from her head, bathe her body and slide into bed. Instantly, she knew her marriage was over.

Cecily had always viewed marriage as sacred. It was her belief that if either partner in the union felt the need to step outside of their vows that it was time to walk away. For her, it was the one unforgivable sin in a marriage. Yet she had lived with Andrew for the past ten years while he stepped out on her with God knows who. She wanted a stable, traditional home for her children. Andrew sucked at being a husband, but there was no denying that he was a great father and that was incredibly important to Cecily. But the fact that she had been driven to look for fulfillment outside of her home confirmed that her marriage was a ticking time bomb and it was only a matter of time before it would be blown to smithereens.

"Well, you're finally up. I guess keeping those late hours is taking its toll on you. Where the hell were you anyway? You've never hung out that late before. And what the hell had you been doing because you came up in here smelling weird as hell? I hope like hell that wasn't a new scent you're thinking of using permanently."

"And good morning to you too, Andrew."

"It's more like afternoon."

"It's only 10:00 and the kids aren't here so I don't see the problem with my sleeping in."

"Okay cool, you got some rest but again where in the hell were you last night?"

"I decided to take myself out to a late movie and then I went for dinner up in Buckhead. It's a shame I have to take myself out because my husband is too busy taking out other women.

"If you want to go out all you have to do is ask. Don't you know you have not because you ask not?"

"First of all, you should stop trying to quote scripture before a lightning bolt sets your ass on fire. Secondly, I don't want to be bothered with you any more than you want to be bothered with me. Let's not kid ourselves into thinking otherwise."

"Yeah, let's not. But please don't think for one second that I believe anything you've just said. You hate eating alone and hate being out alone late at night. So I know damn well you didn't do any of what you said. But it's cool, I'll leave it alone. I won't ask you any more questions and that way you won't have to tell me any more lies."

Cecily breathed a sigh of relief. She didn't care if her little fable was believable or not, she was just thankful that there would be no more questions. She moved about the kitchen gathering the necessary ingredients to prepare a small pot of coffee, bacon, eggs, and toast. She was starving. "Do you want some breakfast?"

"No thank you, I have plans for the day and need to head out."

"What's on tap for you today?"

"Just like I'm not asking you any questions, don't you ask me any."

"Well will you be in early tonight or what?"

"Cecily, I'll be in when I get in. You enjoy the rest of your day." Andrew kissed his wife on the cheek and headed out the door. Cecily wondered where he was going and with whom would he be sharing his day. She thought of calling Karen and questioning her again about whether Andrew had been there spending time with that Hannah chick. But why bother? Cecily knew that Karen would never keep something like that from her in the first place. That is the only reason she had not tried to confront Hannah again after that whole bar incident. Deep in her heart, Cecily knew that Karen would never cover for her husband's affair and she couldn't imagine Hannah sleeping with Andrew and Karen not knowing about it.

Making the decision to put her husband out of her mind for the time being, Cecily finished her breakfast, cleaned her house and before she could decide what to do next her phone rang. "Hello."

"Hey girlie, what are you doing?" Rhonda chirped.

"Nothing much, I was just about to call mom and check on the kids. What about you?"

"I was going to treat myself to a matinee, want to come with me?"

"Sure, I've got nothing else to do. What time does it start?"

"Next show is in two hours. I can pick you up in about forty-five minutes so be ready.

"Okay, see you then." Cecily pushed the button to terminate the call and then let it go again. She listened for the dial tone and began to dial her mother's number. "Hi, Mom how are you guys doing?"

Her mother shared with her their activities of the previous night and how they were preparing to go to the big church picnic and carnival. It was a yearly event that always proved to be a lot of fun. Cecily briefly spoke with her children and then said her goodbyes. With time ticking away, Cecily ran upstairs and put on some more appropriate clothing. Just as she finished dressing her cell phone rang. "Hello."

"Hi beautiful, how are you today?"

A huge smile instantly crept across Cecily's face. "Hello Carter, I'm doing just fine. How are you?"

"I'm decent, could be better if I were still with you. Do you have big plans for the day?"

"I'm going to go catch a movie with my friend Rhonda and maybe a little dinner. What about you? Oh, hold on one second, Carter and let me get the door." Cecily opened the door and waved Rhonda in. "I'm sorry about that, I'm back and I believe you were telling me what you were going to do with your day."

"I actually have a ton of administrative work to catch up on. So I'm going to roll up my sleeves, turn on Sports-Center, and get busy."

"Well try not to work too hard, Mr. Everton."

"I'll do my best. If you want to meet for desert later just call me and we can meet at Café Intermezzo. Their sweets are almost as divine as you."

"Sounds yummy. I'll give you a call later and let you know if that'll be possible, okay?"

"Alright babe, take care and have fun. Bye."

"Okay. Bye-bye." Cecily wasn't even aware of the smile that stretched for miles across her face.

"Who was that?" Rhonda asked with her head cocked to the side like some curious puppy.

"Oh, that was just an old friend I hadn't talked to in a while. You ready?"

"Old friend, huh? Okay. Yeah, I'm ready, let's go."

Still laughing from the foolishness of Tyler Perry's latest film, Cecily and Rhonda pulled out of the theater parking lot and headed towards the Perimeter area. Rhonda had a bad craving for some California Pizza Kitchen. Fortunately it wasn't overflowing with guests and they were seated immediately. Rhonda had dragged Cecily there so much that they both already knew what they wanted. When the waiter approached their table they went ahead and placed their dinner order along with their drink order. They figured there was no point in wasting time.

Rhonda cleared her throat and cautiously proceeded with her line of questioning. "Cecily, we're girls right? Share everything?"

"Of course, it's been that way for years."

"Then I'm going to ask you one more time, who were you talking to on the phone when I got to your house?" I've known you for more than twenty years and no *old friend* has ever made you smile like that."

Cecily breathed deeply as she prepared to tell her best friend the truth. She had already known that Rhonda would bring this up again. That woman could be standing ten miles away and still recognize a lie by the way it hung from Cecily's lips. "I was actually speaking with Carter. I met him in Dr. Douglas' office."

"So is he a patient and if so does he have sickle cell or cancer?"

"He has neither, he actually owns the lab company that draws the blood of Dr. Douglas' patients."

"Why hadn't you told me about him?"

"Rhonda, with so much going on between Andrew and me and worrying about the kids, I guess I really hadn't had time."

"As much as we've been talking? Girl you had time. So is he just a friend or do you have thoughts about him that go far beyond a friendship level?"

"Carter is an awesome guy. He seems to be very kind, thoughtful, and considerate. From what I can see he's an absolute sweetheart."

"I see. Have you seen him outside of the doctor's office?"

"Yes, I actually spent a little time with him last night." Cecily knew what was coming next but she wasn't prepared to tell Rhonda everything that had occurred. Not yet anyway, she was still trying to digest it all herself.

"What did y'all do, Cecily?"

"Just grabbed a bite to eat and watched a movie at his place. It was a very low key evening, a little time to get to know one another."

"Do you have plans to see him again?"

"Gee whiz, Rhonda, I think you're in the wrong line of business. You should have been a detective girl because you are interrogating the hell out of me. But to answer your question, no we haven't made any plans to see each other again."

"Humph," Rhonda's grunted. "Well I certainly hope that you had fun. I see that you're a little uncomfortable talking about this so I'll drop it for now."

"I'm not uncomfortable, there's just not much to tell." Cecily heard herself lie to her best friend and in her heart she knew that Rhonda knew she was lying. She had no idea as to how long she could keep this secret to herself. She'd never done anything like this before and was truly bursting at the seams to tell someone. But the thought of her friend looking at her with disgust and judgment was not something she was prepared to face.

As if reading Cecily's mind, Rhonda blurted, "You know how far back we go. You can tell me anything, Cecily. I love you and I'll understand."

"I know, Rhonda. And you know I trust you with my life. If and when there is something to share, you'll be the first person I run to…I promise."

CHAPTER 10

Hannah moved about the small apartment making sure that everything was neat and clean. She wanted everything in its proper place. She had been raised in a house with a mother that suffered from obsessive compulsive disorder and if things weren't in order her life became a living hell. Regardless of the condition of the house, her mother would arrange and rearrange the homes contents over and over again. But if something wasn't in its assigned spot to begin with, that woman would have a conniption fit. Fortunately Hannah didn't share the disorder, but after years of living with it there were some aspects of it that she couldn't shake.

"Girl, this place looks great. I really lucked out with you as a roommate; you cook and clean like nobody's business. I'm telling you, some man is going to be lucky to have you as a wife."

"Really, Karen, is that all you think about, being someone's wife? I would think that after going through such an ugly divorce, marriage would be the last thing on your mind."

"I wasn't talking about me being married, Hannah. I was simply paying you a compliment," Karen hissed.

"Hell, don't compliment me like that. Marriage is not something I want for the foreseeable future. Every married couple I know seems to be having problems. Either one or both are cheating or it's an abusive marriage or they are simply unhappy with one another. I can't imagine anyone wanting to live in that misery."

"It's not always bad, Hannah. Sometimes people just fail to realize that they were never really meant to be together."

"Yeah, whatever."

"Just remember little girl, life can get pretty lonely. You'll be surprised at the things you may find yourself doing for the comfort of a good man." Karen turned and headed towards her bedroom to finish dressing for the evening.

"Speak for yourself, Karen," Hannah mumbled. She was beyond turned off by Karen's desperation to have a man. Since arriving she had witnessed Karen do things that no woman should resort to. It was downright sad. Hannah would quickly admit that she was no angel and should sometimes show better judgment, but for her there were some lines that should never be crossed.

It wasn't long before both Karen and Hannah were dressed and ready for a good time. The doorbell rang and both ladies made their way to the entrance. With the twist of the doorknob, one woman greeted her date for the night and the other walked out without so much as a goodbye.

CHAPTER 11

Months had passed and Cecily and Andrew seemed to be slipping further and further apart. Their lives together had become so mundane. Everyday Cecily would leave work, pick up the kids, cook dinner, and prepare them for bed. Andrew would come in just in time for dinner, chat with the kids, and retire to his man cave. When the weekends came, he all but disappeared. Funny thing was the neighbors and other associates thought that they were the ideal couple. All they could see was two happy, well adjusted children and a couple that *seemed* happy. No one ever heard any arguing, they didn't realize that it was only because Andrew and Cecily rarely spoke to one another.

This was not the way that Cecily envisioned her life. She was supposed to be married to a man that respected and adored her. Their love and passion for one another was supposed to be stronger than anything that could ever try and come between them. Sadly, there was no passion and the love was as weak as water. At this point, they both realized that they were only together for the sake of the children. And although Cecily was in the midst of an affair of her own, the condition of her marriage still brought tears to her eyes. No, this was not the way it was supposed to be.

Cecily had just slipped into bed when Andrew entered their room. She watched as he undressed and strutted across the floor to the bathroom. He didn't bother to close the door and she continued to watch as he bathed and stepped out of the shower. She was waiting for those old feelings to rise up within her. The feelings she used to get whenever she observed her husband's naked body, but there was nothing. The feelings of lust or desire that used to overtake her had escaped, they were no longer within her reach.

"The kids are going with me this weekend to see my parents," Andrew announced.

"Oh, I'm glad you told me. I'll have all of our things ready Friday afternoon. It'll be nice to see your parents, seems like we haven't gone for a visit in forever."

"You only need to pack Rachel and Brian's things, I figured you'd enjoy some time to yourself."

"But you all never go without me, what will your family think?"

"I already told them that you have to work this weekend and wouldn't be able to make it. There's no need to give any other explanation."

There was no denying that Cecily was hurt by his decision to leave her behind. There were just some things that they always did together despite what may have been going on between them. Trips to Andrew's parents home was always valued family time and they somehow forgot about their issues long enough to enjoy one another during those weekends. Cecily slid down in the bed and wondered how much further apart they could possibly drift without one of them moving out.

"Andrew, how much longer are we going to do this?"

"As long as our children continue to thrive we will be together."

"Do you realize how many smart, successful kids are the products of divorced parents? They can still thrive, be happy, and healthy if we were to part. And to be honest, we really aren't doing them any favors by walking around here like strangers. We aren't able to demonstrate what a loving relationship even looks like. They need to know that they can expect better than we have from their future spouses."

Andrew huffed and flipped over to face his wife. "Well brush up on your acting skills and pretend to be happy because your ass ain't going nowhere. You wanted this expensive house, you got it. You wanted the expensive cars, you got them. We are in too much debt to separate and as much as I have leaving my pockets, I'll be damned if I'm going to be straddled with some outrageous child support order, we both know that half of that money will go in your pocket and not benefit my kids."

"How could you even say that? You know that I am an excellent parent and would do anything for my babies," Cecily retorted with tears rolling from her eyes.

"I'll give you that, you are a good mother, but you are going to have to be a good mother right here in this house with me because I'm not going anywhere and I won't allow you to raise my kids in some cheap ass apartment complex. So turn over, shut up, and go to sleep." Andrew turned his back to Cecily, switched off the lamp and went to sleep.

Cecily eased out of bed and padded down the hall to her office. She quietly closed the door, sat at her desk and began to chart all of her expenses. She jotted down the payment on her vehicle, insurance, credit cards, and an estimate of groceries for the month as well as utilities. She proceeded to add the monthly payment on a small house she had gone to view and calculate the total cost of everything. "Damn it, he's right, I can't afford to go anywhere right now." Cecily dropped her head on her desk and sobbed. She cursed herself for not starting her *just in case* fund earlier and for not adding more to it on a monthly basis.

Years ago, before she was even married, Cecily's mother read her a poem by Maya Angelou that talked about all the things a woman needed, one being enough money to move and survive on her own even if the need never presented itself. Her mother had even given her one thousand dollars to start this fund. But Cecily thought she was in love and turned over the thousand dollars along with everything else she had saved to assist with the down payment on their current home. Sadly, she didn't restart this fund until a year and a half ago and all she'd managed to save was $3,600, not even enough for the down payment on a decent home. But between her individual bills, the expense of her babies, and the utilities that Andrew had delegated to her, it was a little difficult to put away more than her standard $200 per month. But she knew now that she would have to cut some corners and save more.

Two days later, Cecily came home from work and packed a weekend bag for the children. Andrew threw some of his things together and the three of them set out for the two hour drive to his parent's home. A tear fell from Cecily's eye as she watched them drive away. She knew that they would be well cared for, but Andrew leaving without her was just another slap in the face.

The knock on the door startled Cecily. She wasn't expecting company or any deliveries, so she decided to ignore the fact that someone had darkened her doorstep. Cecily turned her attention back to the television, hoping she hadn't missed a pivotal moment in her Lifetime movie. But whoever was at her door wasn't going away and the knocking had turned to pounding. Furious at the nerve of someone trying to break her door down, Cecily took off down the hall, approached the door and screamed, "Who in the hell is banging on my door?"

"Cecily, open this door!" Rhonda demanded with laughter in her voice.

"Girl, what are you doing here?" Cecily asked as she flung her front door open.

Rhonda stepped into the foyer, closed the beautiful wood and glass door, and wrapped her friend in a warm embrace. "I decided to come over because you sounded so sad and pitiful on the phone. I hadn't heard you cry like that in a long time and thought that an evening with your

BFF would be better than you wallowing in self pity and watching some damn Lifetime movie."

"How did you know I was watching Lifetime?"

"Because I know you," Rhonda stated flatly.

"Oh, whatever, come on in and grab a seat. Are you hungry or do you want something to drink?"

"Yes to both so go get dressed and let's go out to dinner." Rhonda could see the objection forming on Cecily's lips and cut her off before the words could escape her mouth. "I'm not taking no for an answer. You don't need to sit here sulking and you have to eat, so get up and make yourself look decent. We'll grab some fake Italian."

"Olive Garden?"

"Yep, now go get ready."

CHAPTER 12

Saturday morning and Cecily lay in bed alone. There was no one waiting for her to cook breakfast, no one asking her to take them to the park or Chuck E. Cheese's. No man asking her where this or that was. Like most women, Cecily enjoyed a little alone time, but this was different. This peace and quiet was not at her request; it was thrust upon her by a man that no longer desired to be in her presence. "Why the hell won't he just let me go?" Cecily mumbled to herself, knowing full well the reasons why.

By noon the house was clean and Cecily was preparing to go and pick up her mom for a little afternoon shopping spree. As she reached for the doorknob, her cell phone rang. One peak at the caller I.D. and a wide smile instantly crept across her face. "Hello there, to what do I owe this pleasure?" She purred as she returned to the couch and took a seat.

"I was hoping that I might be able to coerce you into seeing me this evening."

"And what form of coercion were you going to use, Mr. Everton?"

"Actually, I was just going to ask and if that didn't work I thought I might plead a little bit," Carter confessed with laughter in his voice.

"You'll be glad to know that there is no need for pleading, I'm actually on my own this weekend and would love the company."

"Hmmm... Why is that and for how long?"

"The kid's father decided to take them to visit his parents. Since Monday is a teacher work day, he's not returning with them until mid-morning Monday." Cecily was always careful not to mention her husband's name; in her mind it created more of a separation between the two men in her life.

"Well I don't know about you, but this sounds like breakfast to me. Pack a bag and stay the night with me?"

"I don't know about that, Carter. Do you think that we're ready for all that?" Cecily's real question was if she was ready. As soon as he asked the question, she felt a flutter of butterflies take up residence in her stomach. Since their first encounter, the secret lovers had created three other opportunities to be with one another. Each time seemed to have been better than the last, but overnight may have been pushing the envelope.

"Why wouldn't we be ready? This is an opportunity that we may not get again. I want to spend as much time with you as I possibly can, Cecily. Don't you want the same?"

"Of course I do, but..." Cecily stopped mid-sentence, reflected on her last conversation with Andrew and how he'd left her feeling so empty, so unwanted.

Right now, more than anything, she ached for a man to make her feel wanted…desired. "What time should I arrive?"

"Let's say 7:00pm," Carter responded with an audible smile.

"I'll see you then. Bye." Cecily jumped to her feet, grabbed her keys and headed out of the door. The twenty minute drive to her mother's house seemed to have only taken ten seconds today. Cecily couldn't remember going through the traffic lights or even turning on her mother's street. Her mind was consumed with thoughts of Carter and their impending night together. Just the thought of him sent waves of heat over Cecily's body.

The knock on her car window jarred Cecily from her self induced trance. "Cecily, are you okay? Unlock the door." Her mother's voice was blaring through the glass barrier that separated them. Cecily quickly unlocked the doors and began apologizing as soon as the passenger door was snatched open.

"Are you okay? I saw you pull up ten minutes ago. I assumed you were going to come in and wait for me, but you just sat here like a bump on a log obviously in some sort of trance. I thought something might be wrong with you."

"I'm sorry mom, just got a lot on my mind. I got so caught up in my own thoughts that I didn't even realize I'd been sitting here that long. But I promise, from this point on, you have my undivided attention. Ready to go?"

"Yes, baby, let me grab my purse and lock up. I'll be right back."

Cecily watched as her mother sashayed up the driveway and into her house. She felt an overwhelming need to confide in someone and wondered if that confidant could be her mom. They were extremely close and shared just about everything else, but something told Cecily that her affair couldn't be a topic of conversation for them. Her mother had been a dedicated woman and shared every aspect of her life with only one man. The relationship between her mom and dad was one that they wrote about in romance novels. No, her mom wouldn't get it, wouldn't understand, let alone condone what Cecily was choosing to do. She was almost positive that her mother would be nothing less than appalled by her behavior. She surmised that she'd have to hold on to her secret a while longer.

After about two hours in the mall and a wonderful late lunch at Lavender, mother and daughter were ready to head home. Cecily helped her mom carry her new purchases in the house and then gave her a warm hug goodbye. Next stop, Victoria's Secret. While Cecily had plenty of beautiful lingerie pieces to choose from at home, she wanted Carter to see her in something that no one else ever had. It wasn't long before she found a lovely little chemise that she hoped was the perfect combination of sweet and sexy. Raunchy was not her style and she refused to pretend to be something or someone that she wasn't and something told her that Carter would appreciate that. Unlike her husband, Carter liked her for who and what she was; there was no need to start pretending now.

It was 7:15 and Cecily was at the security gate awaiting entrance into Carter community. She pulled around the corner and was pleased to see him standing outside to greet her. Funny thing was he was in his sweats and Cecily knew that she'd once again have to wait for him to shower and dress. While some folks may have found his routine of dressing after his company had arrived a tad annoying, Cecily thought it was cute. Then again, just about everything he did she found to be cute or endearing.

A light hearted evening with dinner, a movie, and plenty of laughter left all of Cecily's home issues safely tucked away in a very small imaginary box. Truth be told, after calling and talking with her babies earlier in the evening, she had completely put everything and everyone other than Carter out of her mind. They soon returned to Carter's place and the anticipation of what lay ahead for the night caused those damn butterflies to once again make Cecily's stomach their home.

"Are you okay, love?" Carter mused as he stood across the room with a grin on his face.

"Of course I'm fine. Why do you ask?"

"Because you're sitting there looking all cautious. You don't have to wait for me. I want you to do whatever it is that will make you feel more relaxed and at home."

"Oh, I didn't mean to look all uptight. That's certainly not the way I feel. But you know what? I would like to jump in a hot shower."

"By all means, you'll find towels and anything else you might need in the bath."

"Thanks, I won't be long." The hot water melted away any nerves that may have lingered. Cecily slipped into her little satin number, ran her fingers through her hair and was pleased with the reflection that stared back at her.

Carter was relaxing on the bed when she returned to the room and Cecily wasted no time snuggling up to him. It was only a matter of seconds before their tongues began to perform a sultry dance. Carter took his time, his hands caressing her thighs, slowly moving upward until the material that covered her was completely off and scattered about the floor. His kisses trailed south until he reached her breasts. His tongue traced circles around her erect nipples and she moaned with delight as he allowed his teeth to gently graze them. He continued his downward journey until he reached her pulsating passion. Carter buried his face between her legs, licking and sucking as if this were his last meal. Just when Cecily felt that she could take no more, he slowly made his way back up her body and sought refuge for his long, thick, throbbing manhood.

His entry was gentle, but then he changed the game. His strokes were strong, deep, a bit forceful and it felt amazing. Carter moved Cecily from one position to the other. He took her from missionary to doggy style. From sitting in his lap to pinning her against the wall and amazingly, he never broke his stride. Now on her stomach, Carter had a hand full of her hair and was in deep, going harder, deeper, and harder until Cecily exploded with ecstasy. Then, and only then, did he allow himself the pleasure of releasing all that had built up inside.

CHAPTER 13

Andrew returned to the city and immediately took the children to his mother-in-law's house. Cecily was still at work and he had business to take care of before making his way home. It was with much anticipation that he made his way across town to the arms of his lover. They had talked several times over the course of the weekend and she'd described in great detail the things that she wanted him to do to her. This woman was willing to go places and explore techniques that no other woman had ever allowed him to before.

In the beginning, he and Cecily's sex life seemed fine, but he was no fool. He knew that he hadn't been able to completely satisfy her, nor had she been totally satisfying to him. Truth be told, they didn't have the physical chemistry that a married couple should. As the years rolled on, they seemed to go from trying to please one another to simply tolerating each other. Going through the motions just because that's what married folks were supposed to do. It was their duty to one another. Yes, they occasionally had an encounter that was better than most, but those times were few and far between. And for the past few months, they stopped trying all together. Neither wanted to be in the marriage anymore, but like the song says, "It's cheaper to keep her."

Andrew whipped his Acura into a visitor space at the apartment complex. He flipped down the sun visor and took a look at himself in the vanity mirror. As usual, he thought he looked great. No one could ever say that Andrew Connors suffered from poor self-esteem. He glided across the parking lot, climbed the stairs, and knocked on the door.

"Hi Andrew, please come in."

Andrew stepped across the threshold, leaned down, and delivered a gentle kiss on the cheek. "Where is she?"

"She's back there in the room waiting for you. I'm going to make myself scarce; I don't need to be all up in grown folks business."

"Alright then, Hannah, I'll see you later," Andrew chuckled as he made his way back to the master bedroom. He slowly opened the door and was pleased to see his lover waiting for him in a lacy bra, thong and stilettos. "Umm, my caramel Karen, I've been waiting for this all day."

"Come here, handsome," Karen purred.

CHAPTER 14

Rhonda sat across the table from Cecily. They had decided to meet at a little Thai restaurant for lunch. Rhonda couldn't help but notice the distant look in her friend's eyes, she knew that Cecily had been consumed with thoughts that she obviously had not been privy to. She and Cecily had always shared everything and she couldn't understand why her best friend was now keeping her in the dark. Didn't understand why she was keeping secrets.

"I can't take it anymore, Cecily, what in the world has you drifting off to never, never land? I know you've got a lot going on and it might help to let someone in. Let someone share your burden."

"I'm afraid that this is a burden that can't be shared. I have to carry the weight of this alone." Cecily admitted as she dropped her head.

"Please, just talk to me," Rhonda begged.

Cecily shifted in her seat wondering if she could bring herself to tell Rhonda everything. Yes, Rhonda was her girl, her very best friend, but this was a side of her that no one had ever known. This was a side that she herself had never known. Would Rhonda be able to understand without looking at her differently? "I've met someone."

"Do you mean you met a new friend or that you *met someone*?" Rhonda dragged the words out for emphasis.

"I mean I *met someone*. Rhonda, I know it's wrong, but I've been so lonely. My marriage is a joke; my husband treats me like the gum on the bottom of his shoe. But Carter, he treats me like a man should treat a woman. He makes it known that he wants me. He wants to spend time with me, desires me and I love that."

"So, how far has this new found relationship gone?"

The look on Cecily's face revealed where she'd allowed this relationship to go. Tears welled up in her eyes as she began to speak. "I must be losing my mind to allow this to go on. Sadly, I feel no guilt as far as Andrew is concerned. My guilt comes from the kids and how they would view me if this were to ever get out. Trust me, Andrew would make sure to run me through the mud not only to our children, but our families and anyone else that would stand still long enough to listen."

"Well I guess that means that you'll have to be extra careful." Rhonda asserted. She was well aware of all that Cecily had been dealing with and what an ass her husband had been to her. Not to mention the fact that he was caught up in his own affair.

"That's all you have to say?"

"Cecily, you have been dealing with a lot. Everyone who knows you knows that your marriage isn't all that it should be. I'm not saying that what you're doing is right or that I condone it, but I completely understand it. You deserve to have someone make you feel like the queen you are. And let's not forget, Andrew is no angel, he's in the midst of his own little tryst."

"I don't have any proof of that, Rhonda."

"That's easy to fix, we'll just shake it out of Karen. I don't think it'll be too hard to get her to admit that Hannah is knocking boots with your husband."

"Humph, I don't know, she completely shut down at the bar. That girl grabbed Hannah and got the hell on gone. I had never seen her move that fast."

"Yeah well she may have gotten away that night, but not the next time."

"I have to say, Rhonda, I'm a little shocked that she would be willing to protect the relationship between Andrew and Hannah. I'm supposed to be her friend, we've been through a lot together over the years and I've always been there for her. Does she need Hannah's financial contribution so much that she's willing to throw me under the bus?"

"I'm a little surprised myself." Rhonda conceded as she took another gulp of her Thai Tea. "Admittedly I was put off by Karen when I first met her. She always seemed to be chasing what you had. And boy, when you married Andrew, she became almost obsessed with having a marriage like yours. She'd always been so enamored with

Andrew. But then over time, I saw that she really had your best interest at heart."

Cecily rubbed her hands together as though she was torn between prayer and a state of confusion. "I can't figure out why Andrew won't just end this farce of a marriage. I mean, I do understand, it's the money. He doesn't want to have to pay child support and he doesn't want me to have a dime of the savings we've accumulated together, and let's not even talk about the investments. It's not like we're rich or anything, but he wants to be able to penny pinch me to death and keep the great majority for himself. It would be such a help if Karen would just confirm his affair. That would give me the upper hand and the opportunity to lay out my demands and end this crap."

"Cecily, you make a good salary, tell him to keep his damn money and walk away. You and the kids go stay with your mom while you search for a new place."

"Absolutely not! I've pumped plenty into that house and that is the only home my kids have known. The school district is great and they are thriving, I don't want to snatch everything from them."

"Okay, I'm sorry. You're right, the kids belong there and they shouldn't have to leave their home. Rhonda picked up her fork and began to eat, retreating into her own private thoughts. There had to be something that she could do to help her friend, even if Karen refused to step up and do the right thing. Then it hit her, it would take very little investigation to uncover the truth.

Placing her hand over Cecily's, Rhonda spoke softly. "Don't worry girl, I promise it's all going to work out. You deserve to be happy and so do your babies. And I think in time enough will be revealed to set you free. Free and financially secure."

"But how?" Cecily whimpered as tears rolled down her cheeks.

CHAPTER 15

Hannah was more resentful of Karen than she ever knew she could be of any person. The idea of a woman using her painful past against her was almost more than she could bear. When Karen first presented herself to Hannah, it was as a woman that understood her pain. She'd given the impression that she'd walked in Hannah's shoes and understood the hard decisions that she'd had to make. But in time the truth came pouring out, she only reached out to Hannah so that she could use her. She used her for her small monthly stipend, used her as a virtual maid, but most disturbingly, she used her as a cover for her sordid affair. Never having been involved with a married man before, Hannah despised that fact that Karen was forcing her to play the part of the home wrecker.

The slamming door broke Hannah's train of thought and immediately put her on edge. "What the hell is the problem now?" She mumbled to herself. She continued to fold the laundry that was scattered about her bed in hopes that Karen would quietly walk past her room. But no such luck.

"Hey, what are your plans for the evening?" Karen asked breathlessly as she stood in Hannah's doorway.

"What's wrong with you, why are you so out of breath?"

"I ran from the parking lot and up the stairs. I just got a call from Andrew, he wants to see me tonight and I don't have much time to get ready. Now answer *my* question, what are you doing tonight?"

"I'm meeting one of my coworkers for dinner and drinks. She's new to town, seems nice, and I guess we could both use a friend."

"Yeah, okay, whatever, there's a change in plans. I want to cook a nice dinner for Andrew, but I need time to get myself together. Will you please throw us a nice dinner together? You're such a good cook and while you're in the kitchen I can jump in the shower and get all dolled up."

"We haven't even gone shopping; there isn't anything in there to make a good meal out of!" Hannah exclaimed as she thrust her hand towards the kitchen.

"Well duh! That's why there's a change in your plans. Run to the store real quick, grab a couple of steaks or some chicken and turn it into something spectacular."

"You have lost your damn mind," Hannah said matter-of-factly.

With her hand on her hip and a smirk on her face, Karen made a final declaration. "You know what, I was trying to be nice, but this is not a request. Get your ass in gear, go to the store and get to cooking."

A short time later, Hannah found herself pushing a buggy through the aisles of Publix. She hadn't decided what she'd cook, she was still too angry at the fact that she had to do all of this in the first place. Still pondering what to prepare, Hannah was startled when she felt a tap on her shoulder. She jerked around to find herself face-to-face with Rhonda.

"You're Hannah, right?"

"Yes, I am. Do I know you and is there something I can help you with?" Hannah asked politely even though she knew very well with whom she speaking.

"I'm Rhonda; remember we were introduced by Karen a few weeks ago. I didn't mean to scare you, just recognized you and wanted to say hello."

"Oh yes, forgive my absent mindedness. How are you? I haven't had the pleasure of seeing you since the little blow up between me and your other friend, Cecily."

"Yeah, well that was a hot mess, but hey, it's all over with now. What are you doing hanging out in the grocery store on a Friday night?"

"What can I say, the cupboard is bare and I promised Karen that I'd cook tonight." Hannah was surprised to be having this exchange with Rhonda. She assumed that both Cecily and Rhonda hated her after the whole bar fight scene.

"Girl please, let Karen cook for herself. You should be out with some fine guy or at least hanging with your girls."

"I actually did have plans to go out with a coworker, but I cancelled. I didn't want to keep her waiting around on me. She's probably already out getting her drink on."

"Humph, my plans fell through as well. How about you call Karen and tell her to fend for herself, and hang out with me for a while. It was a long day at work and I could use a drink and some good conversation." Rhonda could see Hannah contemplating her offer and was silently willing her to accept. Bumping into her was purely coincidental, but this could be a perfect opportunity to gain information about her connection with Andrew.

Hannah eyeballed Rhonda for a few seconds and then reluctantly accepted her invitation. She was so tired of being under Karen's thumb and figured that Rhonda might not be so bad to hang out with. Lord knows she could use a friend because all she had in Karen was a slave master. "Okay, I live right around the corner. Give me thirty minutes to get changed and I'll meet you."

"Cool, do you know where Mingles is?"

"I sure do," Hannah responded a little more enthusiastically.

"Alright, I'll meet you there; let's just say in an hour."

Rhonda placed her empty buggy back in the stores lobby while Hannah made a mad dash to the deli section. She picked up one of the hot rotisserie chickens, a tub of potato salad, and dinner rolls. One last stop in frozen foods for a bag of steamed veggies, and she was out the door.

Mingles was a nice little dinner club, not overly crowded, and had a great house band providing soothing music. Hannah spotted Rhonda seated at the bar as soon as she walked in the door. She took a deep breath, hoping that she wasn't making a mistake by spending time with Rhonda, and made her way across the room. "Been waiting long?"

"Not at all, I've been here maybe ten minutes. What are you drinking?"

"I'll have red wine." Within seconds a wine goblet was placed in front of Hannah. There was an extended moment of awkward silence where the women pretended to really be engrossed in the music. Hannah took a long sip of courage and decided to break the silence. "So Rhonda, why did you really invite me out?"

Never one to shy away from a question or the truth, Rhonda turned and looked Hannah directly in the eye. "I'm trying to figure out where you're coming from, what you're about, more importantly, if you're screwing my friend's husband."

"Wow, you don't mince words do you?"

Rhonda shrugged her shoulders, "I don't see the point. My mom always taught me to be direct and to never be afraid to speak my mind."

Once again there was an awkward silence. Hannah swirled her drink around in its glass, listened as the band sang their rendition of "Hate On Me" all while she contemplated how she should respond to Rhonda's barrage of inquires. Suddenly, Hannah sat up straight, shoulders back, looked directly at Rhonda and began to speak her truth. Or at least as much of it as she could without giving Karen's dirty little secret away, thus compromising her own situation.

"Rhonda, I can honestly tell you that I have never been involved with a married man. Yes, I date black men, hell I date any man that I have chemistry with, but I draw the line at married men. I'm not about anything deceitful; I'm simply trying to create a new path, a new life for myself here in Atlanta."

"Then can you explain to me how it is that you came to know Andrew and why you lied about having anything to do with him in the first place?"

"It was never my intention to lie to anyone. I very briefly met Andrew one time. I was with Karen, he approached us in a restaurant, we shook hands, said hello and that was it. Of course I thought he was a handsome man, I mean who wouldn't? I didn't mention it because I didn't think that it was significant."

Rhonda looked at Hannah intently as she spoke, carefully listened to every word and surprisingly found herself believing that what she was hearing was the truth. Hannah didn't strike her as the underhanded, conniving, husband stealer she once thought she was. But there still had to be some explanation for Andrew's behavior. He was clearly involved with someone and if not Hannah, then who?

CHAPTER 16

The last two days had been very painful for Cecily and there seemed to be no relief in sight. She'd not been able to make it to work and by Monday afternoon Cecily was on the phone asking Andrew to please come and take her to the emergency room. She made arrangements with her mother to pick up the kids and see after them while she was away.

Four hours later, there was still no sign of Andrew. Not wanting to be carted off by ambulance and knowing that Rhonda was at a weeklong conference, Cecily reluctantly picked up the phone and called Karen.

"Hello," Karen answered as she tried to unsuccessfully clear her voice.

"Hey Karen, it's me Cecily. Did I wake you up?"

"No, no… Something went down wrong, girl and I was trying to clear my throat. What's up?"

"Look, I hate to bother you, but I'm in a great deal of pain and I need a ride to the hospital. Can you please come and pick me up right away? I promise it won't take long."

"Of course I don't mind, but you know you could be waiting in the ER forever."

"I know, I thought of that and that's why I just got off the phone with Dr. Douglas. I don't have to go to the ER, he advised me to go to Direct Admit where they will be waiting for my arrival. All you have to do is drop me off and leave, please."

Karen could hear the distress in her friend's voice and without further hesitation told her that she'd be right there. Karen hung up the phone, rolled over and kissed Andrew. "Baby, I know you thought that she wasn't really sick, but she doesn't sound so good. I'm going to go and run her to the hospital, okay?"

"Fine, you go ahead and take her, I'm going to wait here."

Karen slipped into her clothes, grabbed her purse, and headed for the door. "I'll be back soon, baby."

"Do me a favor and pick up some wings or something on your way back in. I'm starving!" Andrew exclaimed without regard for his wife's health or well being.

ððð

Cecily lay in her hospital bed wondering how her life had gotten so out of control. She never thought she'd see the day when her husband didn't care enough about her to even help her seek medical attention. What had she done to him that was so horrible? What had she done to deserve his hatred? More importantly, why was she deserving of this debilitating disease, this unbearable pain?

Finally after three attempts to start an I.V., the needle had successfully been placed and Cecily's pain was being alleviated by the intravenous dose of Dilaudid she'd received an hour ago. The strong medication caused her to drift off into a sound sleep. She was totally unaware of Carter's presence. He'd heard the office nurse phone in all of Cecily's initial hospital orders from Dr. Douglas. He'd actually gone over to the hospital an hour after hearing the call and was surprised to see that she hadn't checked in yet. Then he determined that she must have been making arrangements for her children. But it didn't take him long to decide that he'd return later that same evening.

Carter sat quietly on the small sofa working on his laptop. He was unaware that Cecily had awakened and was watching him. She was pleased to see that she was not alone, but the fact that her company was Carter simply thrilled her.

"Hey you." She spoke in a groggy voice.

"Hey yourself," Carter replied as he placed his computer on the sofa and jumped up to move closer to Cecily's bedside. "How are you feeling, love? Do you need me to get you anything?"

"No, your being here is all I need. How long have you been waiting for me to wake up?"

"I've only been here an hour or so. I was a little concerned that my being here might cause issues for you if your significant other came back for an evening visit."

"Trust me, that's not going to happen. He wouldn't even come home and give me a ride up here. I thought I was going to have to call an ambulance, but finally, I was able to reach one of my girlfriends. Karen ran over, picked me up and dropped me off."

"I know I'm not supposed to talk about your husband, but that's a sorry son-of-a-bitch. I don't care what kind of problems y'all are having; he shouldn't be treating you like this. For all he knew, you could've been at deaths door. And I appreciate your girl giving you a ride, but damn, she couldn't stay with you for a little while, at least until they put you in a room?"

"It's no big deal. The important thing is that I'm here getting the care that I need and trust me, the people that matter are here by my side." Cecily reached out and took Carter by the hand. She knew that he meant well, but his words were a hurtful reminder of the pitiful turn her life had taken.

"You're right and I'm sorry, enough of that. Are you hungry?"

"As a matter of fact I am. I would love some pizza."

"Your wish is my command. I'll run out and grab us a pizza and a couple of drinks. I won't be gone long at all." Carter grabbed his keys and headed out of the door as Cecily's nurse came in.

"How are you feeling Mrs. Connors?"

"I'm okay, just a little achy, but I'm trying to be a trooper."

"What is your pain level on a scale of one to ten with ten being the worst?"

"I'm probably at about a five right now."

"Well I'd be happy to get you something for pain. I don't advise you to let it get any worse."

"I really don't want to go back to sleep right now, is it possible for me to have just half of my normal dosage?"

"Sure, I can do that. Dr. Douglas ordered four milligrams of Dilaudid, but you just want two, correct?"

"Yes please." The nurse left the room and returned a couple of minutes later with the needle containing the strong narcotic. She administered the drug and Cecily instantly felt its affects. While it made her drowsy, it didn't completely take her over like the full four milligram dosage did. With the smaller dose, she was able to stay in better control of her faculties.

With pizza and sodas in hand, Carter came strolling back into Cecily's hospital room. She woke from her brief nap and enjoyed the casual meal and great conversation with her lover. Carter then pulled out a DVD, popped it in the player that the hospital had bolted to the television stand and eased into the small bed with Cecily. They snuggled, watched the movie, but mostly enjoyed being close to one another. Cecily felt so much better just knowing that there was actually someone that cared for her, her health and well being after all.

CHAPTER 17

Rhonda sat at the kitchen counter watching Cecily prepare brunch and trying to absorb what her friend had just shared. "So you're not kidding with me, Andrew really didn't check on you or the kids the entire week?"

"I am not lying. I was hurting like hell and not only would he not come and take me to the hospital, but he didn't come and visit me once or even go to my mom's house to check on the kids. She said that he called over there to ask if they needed anything, she said no and that was the last she heard from him. My babies were so happy to see me; it was almost as if they thought they'd never see either of their parents again."

"Well listening to them play in there now, you'd never know they had a worry in the world. By the way, where is Andrew this morning?"

"He was up and gone early this morning. He promised the kids that he'd be back this afternoon to take them to the movies and for pizza. So far he hasn't broken any promises to them; let's hope he doesn't start today." Cecily pulled four plates from the cabinet and four juice glasses. Rhonda poured the juice while Cecily piled the plates full of sausage, eggs with cheese, and blueberry muffins. "Rachel, Brian, come on guys and let's eat."

Cecily's children gobbled up their food. Their mom's homemade muffins were their absolute favorite. "I love Grandma and her cooking, but nothing beats being here with you and eating your food, Mom." Rachel proclaimed with a stuffed mouth.

"Yeah, Mom, me too," Brian chimed.

"You too what, Brian?" Rhonda asked, clearly amused by her god kids.

"You know, Aunt Rhonda, what Rachel said."

Everyone finished their meal and the kids ran off to go clean their rooms. Rhonda got up and began to clean the kitchen and insisted that Cecily remain seated. Placing the dishes into the dishwasher, Rhonda began speaking slowly. "I didn't tell you about my evening out did I?"

"What evening out?"

"Before I left for the conference, I bumped into a mutual acquaintance at the grocery store and we ended up hanging out together. It surprisingly turned out to be a pretty good night."

"Oh, who was it?"

"Hannah," Rhonda said bluntly as she lifted her eyes to meet Cecily's gaze. Rhonda leaned against the counter, wiped her hands, and began to explain. "I bumped into her at Publix after my plans with this dude were cancelled. I approached her and she tried to pretend that she didn't remember me, but I knew she was faking it. Thinking I could drag some information out of her, I invited her to join me for drinks. I couldn't believe she accepted."

"We met at Mingles and didn't mince words. I came right out and asked her if she was involved with Andrew. Cecily, she was just as direct when she said that she'd briefly met Andrew, but had never messed with a married man. We know that he's screwing someone, but my gut tells me that Hannah is telling the truth."

"I don't know what to think, Rhonda. She didn't come off to me as the most upstanding chick in the world when I met her. And the way she spoke to me about Andrew, I have no faith in anything that she says."

The front door slammed shut and Andrew moved hastily through the house. He entered the kitchen, looked around, and finally decided to speak. "Hey y'all. What's up, Rhonda?"

Rhonda cocked her head to the side and answered very dryly, "Nothing."

"Are the kids ready to go?"

Cecily turned and faced Andrew with such a look of disgust in her eyes that it made him turn away. "Yes, they should be ready. How long will you all be gone?"

"Why, do you have plans?"

"I have errands and I want to make sure I'm back when they get back. I can't chance you being in such a hurry to get out of here that you leave them alone for any length of time."

"When the hell have I ever left these children home alone?"

"You never have, but your behavior has become so unpredictable that I'm not taking any chances. Only God knows what you may do next."

"You can be a simple bitch when you want to be, you know that?"

"That's right. Make yourself feel like a big man by calling me names. Now, answer my question, how long will you be gone?"

"Not long enough for you to go run the streets late into the night."

"That's your method of operation, not mine. I'm here being a full time parent, cooking, cleaning, helping with homework, tucking our children into bed while you're out running the streets sleeping with only God knows who."

"Then you're doing the job that you were placed on this Earth to do. Now if I could get you to screw me the way you're supposed to, then your mission in life would be complete."

"You are such an ass; I swear I almost hate you now. And you don't ever have to worry about me screwing you again. I don't know where you're putting that little raggedy dick of yours or what you may have contracted, but I do know that you won't be giving it to me. All I want from you now is a freaking divorce."

"Keep dreaming, bitch."

Cecily jumped up, grabbed a knife from the butchers block and lunged at Andrew. "Call me bitch one more time and I swear I'll cut your fucking throat!"

Rhonda ran from behind the counter to grab her friend but wasn't able to make it to her before Andrew knocked the knife from her hand and pimp slapped her across the face. "Bitch, don't you know that I will kill you? Don't you ever try no shit like that with me."

"Daddy, don't you hit my mommy! Rachel screamed with tears running down her face.

Andrew turned to see his daughter crying and immediately regretted laying hands on Cecily. Deep in his heart, he knew that he'd provoked the entire situation and was wrong in every way. This was not the example he wanted to be for his children. He walked over to Cecily and pulled her into a gentle embrace. "I'm so sorry, Cecily. I am so very sorry."

Looking out the corner of her eye, Cecily saw her daughter watching closely and that is the only reason she didn't push Andrew away from her. Instead she allowed him to apologize over and over again.

Once everything had calmed down, Andrew left with the kids. Cecily and Rhonda gathered their things in preparation to run their errands. "Can you believe he hit me like that?" Cecily asked still in a state of disbelief.

"I'm surprised that he didn't beat your ass into the ground. Cecily, I don't care how mad you get; you don't go around pulling knives on people unless you're ready to use them, understand?"

CHAPTER 18

Carter's townhouse is where Cecily chose to seek refuge from Andrew and the stresses of her day-to-day life. Carter was her comfort. He made her happy and she felt completely at peace when she was with him, and tonight was no different. She'd been afforded the opportunity to spend some quality time with whom she considered the great pleasure releaser in her life. And the pleasures went far beyond just the physical. He understood her, allowed her to be herself, accepted, and loved her for whom and what she was. Or at least that's the feeling she got from him, and she reveled in it.

"So tell me what's on your mind, love? When we talked the other day you were so upset, I could tell you'd been crying. You said you'd tell me what the problem was, but here we are days later and I still don't know what was wrong?" Carter stroked Cecily's hair while he waited for her response.

She opened her mouth to speak but quickly closed it shut. Cecily took an extra moment and decided that telling him about the physical altercation might not be the wisest thing in the world. "There was a big blow up at home. There seems to forever be an argument, some kind of fight, but sadly my daughter witnessed this one and became very upset."

Carter sat up in a more upright position. "When you say fight, does that mean that things have gotten physical? Cause I swear, if fists are flying I *will* go over there. Damn everything else, we'll just have to be found out. But I will go over there if that dude ever lays a hand on you."

In that moment, Cecily was so glad that she'd not divulged all that had happened and opted to tell her lover a little white lie. "No, that's something you don't have to worry about. He knows better than to put his hands on me."

Carter laid back down, satisfied with Cecily's response. "Well it won't be much longer. Are you still planning to make changes after the holidays?"

"I am, they are fast approaching, but yes, I still plan on making big changes after the New Year. I initially said that I didn't want to move the kids out of the only home they've ever known, but I just can't keep up this charade anymore. I am miserable and life is too short for me to be this unhappy on a continuous basis. So, I have a realtor looking for me a nice, but modest home and I'm forging ahead."

"I know you want to be free of that situation and trust me, I want you free of it, but I still think that you should fight for your home. That's something that you deserve for both you and your children."

"Yes, I know. I guess we'll just have to see how everything works out. But speaking of holidays,

Thanksgiving is in two weeks, what are your plans for the holiday?"

"I decided to go back up north and spend a little time with my parents, catch up with some old friends. I'll be flying out the end of next week and returning the Sunday after Thanksgiving. Think you can make it that long without me and not go crazy?" Carter teased.

"Oh my, I don't know. That's a long time, hope I don't end up in a corner pulling at my hair and calling your name over and over."

"Speaking of calling my name over and over..." Carter moaned seductively as he pulled Cecily on top of him and let nature take its course.

CHAPTER 19

"Where the hell do you think you're going?" Karen demanded.

"I'm going home to visit my mom for the holidays. Christmas is in two weeks and school is out. I haven't had a chance to spend time with her in quite a while. So, I'm off to Kansas City and I'm excited about it." Hannah never stopped packing. She was constantly moving about the room, gathering her things and tossing them into bags. She'd already predicted that Karen would have a little conniption fit, but she didn't give a damn. Nothing or no one was going to stop her from spending this time with her mother.

Karen snatched a blouse from Hannah's hand. "Look, I need you here. I want to spend as much time with Andrew as possible and you know that you're supposed to be my decoy. You're the one he's sneaking around with, remember? Or at least that's what we want Cecily to believe. I need you to keep suspicions on you and Andrew, this was part of our arrangement, damn it."

"I never agreed to let your sick little game consume my entire life. I was stuck here during Thanksgiving; you're not ruining my Christmas break too. I'm sure you'll figure something else out," Hannah spat back as she snatched her shirt back and threw it in the suitcase.

"Just don't forget, you little murderer, I'm the reason your raggedy ass is walking the streets a free woman. You *will* show your appreciation!"

"Not by staying here for the holidays I won't. I will see you the day after the New Year. Bye!" Hannah grabbed her bags, bumped her way through the modest apartment and slammed the door behind her.

Furious, Karen picked up a crystal picture frame holding a picture of Hannah's mom and threw into the bedroom wall. The shattered pieces flew all over the place as Karen cursed her roommate's name.

The airport was packed, but Hannah spotted her mom right away waiting for her at the baggage claim. She pushed her way through the crowd and into the open arms of her mom. No words were immediately spoken, instead, they stood there crying and swaying from side to side. Onlookers would have sworn that Hannah was just returning from war.

Riding through the city brought back so many memories and filled Hannah with such joy. Only a few more miles until they reached the house and she'd already imagined the feast that her mom had prepared. Jesse Graham, Hannah's mom, was known for her great cooking skills and she did not disappoint her daughter. Crossing the threshold of the small, red brick, three bedroom home Hannah was greeted by the smell of blackened salmon, sautéed vegetables, roasted red potatoes, and freshly made yeast rolls. "I pulled the rolls out of the oven right before I walked out of the door to pick you up. Everything should still be good and hot for my baby girl."

"Mom, you are the best. I have missed you so much and I intend to enjoy these next few weeks with you to the fullest. Who knows, I may even cook for you once or twice," Hannah said with a smile as she took a seat at the glass top table.

"Now I would enjoy that. Everybody is always looking for me to do all the cooking, but I never get invitations to enjoy someone else's home cooked meal." Jesse sat a plate full of food in front of her daughter and sat one down for herself. She grabbed a couple of glasses of cola and sat down to break bread with the person she loved most in the world.

"Mom, this is delicious, I swear I could make a meal off of these rolls alone."

"I'm glad you like it, Hannah. So tell mama what's been going on with you. How are you doing in school?"

"I'm doing really well; can you believe that I'm at the top of my class?"

"That's awesome! If you keep that up, you shouldn't have any problems finding a job after you graduate. Nurses are in such high demand right now, I'm sure you'll be paid top dollar."

"From your lips to God's ears. My only concern is that my record may hold me back. I really want to work in a hospital setting, but I think that I may end up in a doctor's office somewhere instead."

"Why is that?"

"It's a criminal record, Mom. I may not ever be able to get past it."

"You will, watch what I tell you. It will not be a stumbling block for you forever, Hannah. Now what about your parole officer friend, isn't she helping you with everything? I thought she was going to try and help you get your record expunged?"

Almost immediately Hannah's eyes filled with tears. She dropped her head, ashamed that she'd allowed herself to get tangled up in the mess that Karen was creating. "Mom, it's all such a mess. That parole officer is my roommate, and the demands that she's putting on me are unbearable." Hannah broke down into all out sobs. Tears were flowing and the thought of what Karen wanted her to ultimately do caused her physical pain.

Jesse ran around the table, fell to her knees, and embraced her child. "Go ahead and cry, get it all out. Let those tears cleanse your soul, honey. Mom is right here for you and whatever the problem is, we will figure it all out."

"Thank you, Mom. But I think that I'm just at the mercy of this mad woman." Hannah sat up and grabbed a paper towel to dab her face and blow her nose. "Sit here and let me explain." She motioned for her mom to sit in a chair right beside her. "So you know that I had a three year parole sentence to complete once I was released from prison right?"

"Of course." Jesse watched her intently, hanging on every word.

"Well, I messed up. I neglected to check in with my P.O. on a regular basis like I was supposed to. It didn't seem like a problem. She was real cool whenever I would show up and told me to just make sure that I checked in at least once every eight weeks or so. So that's what I did and everything was going smoothly. Then I show up one day and she shows me a file with all of my information in it including every missed appointment. Told me that she had enough to prove I'd failed to meet the requirements of my parole and she would send me back to prison unless I did what she wanted."

"And exactly what does this extortionist want?"

"She's sleeping with her best friend's husband and wants me to pretend to be having an affair with him in an effort to keep suspicion off of her. But ultimately, she wants me to kill her friend so that she and the husband can marry." Hannah began to cry all over again.

"You have got to be kidding me. What in the hell makes her think that you're capable of taking another person's life? This woman must be crazy!"

"Mom, she knows that I've already killed once and in her mind, it shouldn't be a big deal for me to do it again."

"Hannah, you didn't kill anyone in cold blood. You were in a fight for your life. Everyone knows that that man was trying to rape you. He'd already beaten you and you had the bruised and bloody face to prove it."

"Yes, but with the bullet in his back the judge felt that I had an opportunity to get away without resorting to using a deadly weapon."

"Did you explain to her that you shot him in the back because that was your only chance to save yourself? He was reaching for a weapon of his own, had you not pulled the trigger, you would be the one that died."

"I know that and you know that. The problem is that I let that stupid attorney talk me into letting a judge decide my fate instead of having a jury trial. The judge didn't see things my way and now I'm faced with the choice of killing an innocent woman or going back to prison. Mom, those were the hardest three years of my life. I can't go back."

CHAPTER 20

The Christmas holidays had been a difficult time of year for Rhonda ever since her parents passed away six years ago. Her mother had battled lung cancer for a little over a year before it had taken her life. Her father had been an amazing care taker to her mom and literally grieved himself to death within five months of her passing.

Growing up as an only child, her parents always went all out for Christmas. It was their attempt to make up for the fact that they hadn't been able to give her a sibling, another person to share all the things that brothers and sisters shared. Yes, she had cousins that she was very close with, friends that spent the night and all, but it still wasn't the same. She had once asked her parents about adopting a child, but her mother didn't utter a word. She simply looked at Rhonda's father and he very sternly said that it was not an option and was not to be discussed again. And it never was. Instead, her parents kept her involved in all kinds of extracurricular activities, played with her as if they were kids themselves sometimes and made each Christmas season more spectacular than the last.

Since their passing, Rhonda had spent most of her holidays with other family members or friends, but this year she decided to go it alone. Nothing she did seemed to put her in a celebratory mood and she didn't see the point in going to someone's house just to serve as a wet blanket. So it was Christmas Eve and Rhonda was on her way to the store for a bottle of wine. As she pulled up to a traffic light, she noticed that the car in the other lane was just like Andrew's. As the car pulled off, she glanced at the tag and his vanity plate gave him away, it was indeed Andrew. Instead of turning in the store parking lot, she allowed one car to get in between her and Andrew and then proceeded to follow him. This was not his side of town and she couldn't imagine why he wouldn't be at home with his family preparing to play Santa Clause for his kids.

It only took a couple of turns before Rhonda realized exactly where Andrew was headed…Hannah's. And to think, she believed Hannah when she swore to her that she was not seeing Andrew. She had allowed herself to be totally sucked into Hannah's whole "I'm innocent of the accusations" routine. She trusted that Hannah was telling her the truth when she said that she wasn't, nor had she ever been involved with a married man, including Andrew.

Rhonda pulled her car into a space near the front of the apartment entrance and watched from across the lot as Andrew exited his car and glided up the stairs to his waiting lover. But it wasn't Hannah that opened the door, it was Karen. Rhonda's mouth dropped open in disbelief as she watched her friend welcome another woman's man into her home. She couldn't understand why Karen would allow one of her best friend's husbands to use her house to carry on this disgraceful affair. What in the world could Hannah have over Karen? It would have to be some very damaging information in order to force Karen to be a part of this unbelievably deceptive behavior.

"What should I do? What should I do?" Rhonda asked herself over and over again. She bit her lip as she contemplated what her next move should be. "I don't want to call Cecily with this, not tonight. She's with the kids and that's where she needs to stay." She began to tap her fingers against the cold window as she weighed her options. "Should I go bang on the door and surprise everybody or just leave and tell Cecily about it later? Lord please give me a little direction here?"

Try as she might, Rhonda couldn't force herself to drive away and deal with it all at a later time. Instead, she climbed out of the car, walked briskly through the parking lot and up the stairs. Rhonda took a deep breath and began to knock on the door. Three taps and no response. She'd come this far and wasn't going to be ignored so she balled up her fist and began to bang as if she were trying to knock the door down.

"Who the hell is it?" Karen shouted from the other side of the door.

"It's me, Rhonda. Open the door; I need to talk to you."

"Can't it wait until tomorrow? I'm busy and can't really talk right now." Karen spoke in a softer voice.

"No, Karen, I have to talk to you right now!" Rhonda's voice was forceful, so much so that her tone actually scared Karen a little. The lock clicked and the door was cracked just enough to allow Rhonda entrance. "What the hell are you thinking? How could you, Karen? Cecily is supposed to be your friend."

"Rhonda, why are you here and what in the world are you babbling about?"

"Don't try to play stupid with me, Karen. I would respect you a whole lot more if you were woman enough to own up to your part in all of this."

Tugging at her robe, Karen looked at Rhonda as if she could kill her with her bare hands. "I don't know what you *think* is going on here, but I would appreciate it if you would leave my house."

"I tell you what; I'll leave as soon as Andrew leaves. You go drag his sorry ass out of Hannah's bed and I'll walk out right behind him." The expression on Karen's face totally changed and it signaled to Rhonda that things were not quite as she'd imagined them to be. "He is in Hannah's room, isn't he?"

"Of course he is!" Karen barked with great annoyance. "But surely you don't expect me to barge in there and break up whatever they are in the middle of? I have no desire to see their bare asses."

"Fine, I'll go get him. If you've seen one ass you've seen them all." Rhonda spun around and started to march off through the apartment, but Karen immediately blocked her path.

"Look, he's a grown man, she's a grown woman and we should stay out of their business. Now would you please just leave?" Karen was almost begging.

"I tell you what, let me make a quick call and I'm outta here." Rhonda whipped out her cell phone and dialed Hannah's number. Surprisingly, when her phone rang she didn't hear it in the apartment. "Hey! Merry Christmas to you too. Umm, where are you? Oh okay, well I'll see you when you get back. Bye." Without another word, Rhonda drew her fist back and punched Karen in the mouth. "You sorry ass bitch, that's your best friend's husband in your bed!" Rhonda continued to whale on Karen as she struggled unsuccessfully to get back on her feet.

"That's enough!" Andrew shouted as he pulled Rhonda off of his lover. He picked up Rhonda's purse and keys and threw them out the front door. Without regard for her cursing and screaming, Andrew grabbed Rhonda by the hair and jacket collar and threw her out as well.

CHAPTER 21

Rhonda was invited over to Cecily's mom's house for Christmas, just as she had been every year for the past several years. But she decided to stay home, lick her wounds, and ponder when and how to tell Cecily that her trifling husband was sleeping with her equally trifling friend. Yes, Rhonda was well aware of the fact that Cecily had taken a lover of her own, but she also reasoned that this was something Cecily was pushed into. Andrew was anything but a loving and compassionate husband. He'd been treating his wife like crap for a long time and quite frankly, Cecily deserved better.

There was absolutely nothing on television except for Christmas movies and Rhonda refused to watch those. Instead, she decided to watch a few of the DVD's she'd purchased over three months ago and never got around to watching. Just as she was about insert *Crazy Stupid Love* into the player the phone rang. "Hello."

"Hey, what are you doing?" Cecily sang into the phone.

"I was just about to watch a movie. How did the kids like their gifts from Santa this morning?"

"Oh my goodness, they loved everything! They were so excited, you should have seen them ripping the paper off of their gifts. They also loved the gifts from Auntie Rhonda. You should come over to Mom's for a while. That way they can thank you in person instead of a stupid phone call later."

"Thanks for the offer, Cecily, but I'll take the phone call. Like I told you before, I'm just not with it this year and I don't want to bring you guys down. And I'm sure that Andrew would appreciate not having your friends hanging around for the holiday."

"Girl please, I haven't seen Andrew. He called and spoke to the kids, gave me some B.S. story about getting stranded and his brother picked him up so he decided to spend the night and Christmas day with his family. Can you believe that? His sorry behind didn't even care about seeing his kids on Christmas. So I packed up the kids and we came to Mom's last night. This is where Santa brought us all of our gifts."

"You have got to be kidding me?"

"I kid you not. Now come on…" Cecily was cut off mid-sentence and the next voice Rhonda heard on the line was Mama Shirley's, Cecily's mom.

"Rhonda, baby I want you to do Mama Shirley a favor and get up, put some clothes on and get over here for dinner."

"But Mama Shirley I…"

"No ma'am, no excuses. Mama will see you in about an hour. Love you, bye."

And just like that, Mama Shirley laid down the law and hung up the phone. Rhonda pulled herself up from the couch and headed for the bedroom to get dressed in something a little more appropriate for Christmas dinner. Forty-five minutes later, she was walking out the door and trying to mentally prepare herself to be around her friend without giving a hint as to the things she knew about her husband and her other best friend.

"There's my girl!" Mama Shirley exclaimed as she opened the door and pulled Rhonda into a warm embrace before she even had a chance to reach for the doorbell. "Come on in, we're just about to sit down for dinner."

Rhonda went right in, greeted everyone with hugs and began to help set the table and serve up the delicious food that Mama Shirley had lovingly prepared. It was a feast fit for a king. She'd cooked everything; turkey and dressing, macaroni and cheese, candied yams, greens, ham, potato salad, and of course, her famous sweet potato pies. One whiff of that food and Rhonda was glad she'd gotten up and made her way over.

"This is delicious and so much better than sitting at home alone watching movies. Thank y'all for calling me, I really enjoyed dinner. I swear I've just gained ten pounds."

"Rachel and Brian, are you guys full? Did you have enough?" Cecily asked her kids with the sweetest smile on her face.

Brian nudged Rachel and she replied for the both of them. "Yes ma'am, but if you want to give us one more slice of pie we'll take it."

"I bet you would, but sorry, no more sweets. Why don't you guys go and play with your toys while the adults talk and clean up, unless you want to clean up?"

"Oh no, we're out of here." The kids jumped up and scampered away to the back of the house. Rhonda looked around the table at the dishes that remained. Even with the scraps of food that littered the plates, the china pattern was beautiful. The gold trimmed plates were adorned with soft pink and ivory flowers. The china had been purchased many years ago when Mama Shirley was a new wife, creating a new home for her and her husband. But it was only used on special occasions and after all this time, it still looked new. Rhonda stood up and was about to start clearing the table when Mama Shirley gently grabbed her by the wrist and pulled her back down to her seat.

"Baby, these dishes can wait. Sit and talk with us for a little bit. You've been pre-occupied since you got here. Tell us, what's swirling around in that pretty little head of yours?"

"Don't you know that this thing is as empty as a crack heads bank account?" Rhonda teased as she pointed at her temple.

Cecily placed her hand on top of Rhonda's as she tried to coerce her into sharing her troubles. "Come on, Rhonda, stop playing. I've known you forever and it's obvious when there is something weighing heavily on your mind. Tell us what's going on, maybe we can help."

Rhonda pulled her hand away from Cecily's gentle grip and contemplated if she should potentially ruin the rest of the holiday with the truth. But if she didn't speak up, both Cecily and Mama Shirley would hound her until she came up with something believable. So without further hesitation, she let the truth flow. "I know where Andrew spent Christmas and it wasn't with his family."

"Girl, you don't think I know that? I'm sure that he and Hannah have had a fabulous holiday together."

Rhonda dropped her head and mumbled, "No, he's had a fabulous holiday with Karen."

"What did you say?"

"He's with Karen, she's the one he's been having the affair with, not Hannah."

"Karen would never do that to me; we've been friends far too long and have been through too much together for her to do something like that to me." Tears filled Cecily's eyes and her voice trembled as she spoke her disbelief of the situation. "How do you know and are you positive?"

"I saw Andrew's car on that side of town last night and decided to follow him just to confirm our suspicions. I saw Karen open the door for him and couldn't believe that she was actually allowing him and Hannah to carry out their affair in her presence." Rhonda was trying to be very matter-of-fact as she recounted the events of the previous evening. She didn't want to display any emotion but was unable to remain stone faced. Tears threatened to fall from her eyes. "I banged on the door and demanded Karen let me in. When she did I got on her case about the situation and started yelling for Hannah to come out. When Hannah never answered, I pulled out my cell phone and called her. That's when I discovered that she was out of town. Once the realization of the situation hit me, I became so angry that I pounced on Karen. We fought until Andrew pulled me off and literally threw me out of the apartment. That's how I got these lovely scratches all across the back of my neck." Rhonda lifted her reddish brown hair to expose the mess of scratches and bruises left by Andrew.

Mama Shirley had moved her chair closer to Cecily and was now holding her child in her arms. Cecily didn't even try to control her emotion; she was clearly hurt and didn't stifle her sobs. "Mama is here, baby. You let it out, let it all out."

"I knew he was cheating, that was no secret, but with Karen. How could he? Did he choose her just as a way to add insult to injury? He knows how close we were. And Karen, I don't even know what to say about her now."

"She's always been jealous of you and Andrew's marriage, Cecily. Think about it, everything that's ever come out of her mouth has been about what a good man Andrew is and how lucky you are." Rhonda reminded Cecily of Karen's past comments. "And no matter the disagreement you had with Andrew, she always took his side, defended him. Always saying that you were too hard on him."

"It's just disgraceful!" Mama Shirley hissed. "I'm not a violent woman, but if I could get my hands on that Karen I'd put a beating on her she wouldn't soon forget."

"How am I supposed to face him, to deal with him without acting a fool in front of my kids?" Cecily pondered as she tried to wipe the tears that wouldn't stop flowing.

CHAPTER 22

Andrew parked his car close to the curb of the tree lined street. He looked around and took notice of the fact that for a Christmas day there were very few kids playing outside with their new toys. When he was a kid, Christmas day found all of the neighborhood children riding their new bikes or playing with their new balls or other toys outside. But in this age of electronics, he was sure that all of the kids, including his own, were stuck in front of televisions with game controllers in their hands.

Looking at the tan stucco ranch styled home, Andrew contemplated how big of a scene he would be walking into if he tried to go and see his children. He knew beyond a shadow of a doubt that Cecily would not return home today, but it was Christmas and there was no way that he was going to let the entire day go by without seeing them. He eased out of the car and took slow, steady steps up the walkway to the front door. Andrew took another look around, closed his eyes and tried to ask God to not let this turn into a disaster, lifted his hand and rang the doorbell. It seemed like an eternity, but within a minute the door opened and Cecily stood before Andrew as if she were ready for war.

"What the hell are you doing here?" She hissed.

"It's Christmas, I came to spend a little time with the kids. I've never been away from them on the holidays." Andrew spoke in a very low, calm, respectful tone.

"You had the chance to spend last night with them as well as all day today, but instead you chose your whore over your children. So you go back to that trick because the kids don't need you or miss your ass." Cecily attempted to slam the door in his face, but Andrew put his hands up and pushed the door back open.

"What the hell! You can't just force your way up in here, this is not your home and you are not welcome." Cecily shouted louder than she wanted, drawing the attention of not only her mom and Rhonda, but the children as well. Rhonda was the first one at the door threatening to call 911. Mama Shirley tried unsuccessfully to block the kids, but wasn't able to contain them once they spotted their dad at the front door. Rachel and Brian pushed their way passed their grandmother and into the arms of their father.

"Daddy, where have you been? Where were you last night? You never showed up for Christmas Eve so we came over here. You've missed dinner and everything. Where were you?" As always, Rachel was full of questions. Brian didn't care about any of the whys or where's, he was just glad to see his father. "Daddy, do you hear me, where were you?" Rachel demanded.

"Yes, Andrew, where were you? Your daughter wants to know," Cecily chimed sarcastically.

Ignoring his wife, Andrew knelt down and spoke lies to his daughter. "Daddy had a lot of work to take care of, baby girl. I'm so sorry I wasn't home with you guys last night, but I'm here now. You guys want to show me what Santa brought you?"

"No!" Cecily protested, but before she could continue her argument, Mama Shirley decided to be the voice of reason.

"Yes, Andrew, come on in and go to the back room with the kids. Spend a *little* time with them and then you'll need to leave." She said very matter-of-factly. Mama Shirley then ushered everyone back into the house and closed the door.

"Mama, how are you just going to invite him in like this against my wishes, especially knowing what and who he was doing last night?" Cecily cried her frustration with her mother's decision.

"Andrew, you don't have a lot of time so I suggest you stop listening to us and go on to the back with your children." Mama Shirley watched as Andrew made his way down the hall while simultaneously grabbing Cecily by the arm and dragging her into the kitchen. "Cecily, you and that man are already traveling a bumpy road. From the look of things, it's about to get a whole lot bumpier. You have got to make sure to control yourself around those babies; they can't see you popping off like some crazy woman. And you can't deny him access to his children. If or when this ends up in court, you'll need to be seen as the better parent if you want full custody of Rachel and Brian. Don't forget, he's an attorney with connections.

Don't give him a reason to try and get you out of the kid's lives." Mama Shirley was advising her daughter based on her long career as a paralegal in a divorce attorney's office. "I know your emotions are all over the place right now, but these are the kind of things you have to think about now. Under no circumstances are you to bad mouth him around the kids and please don't allow them to be used as pawns in whatever war you two decide to wage against one another. And Cecily, before you do or say anything else to him, please pray about it first."

Cecily hugged her mom and wept silently. Her mother was the wisest woman she'd ever known and knew that she needed to heed every word her mom said. "I know you're right, Mom, but I'm so angry, I want to hurt him so badly."

"I know you do, sweetie. I know that anger and that's why I want you to pray. God can take that anger away from you and replace it with an unshakable sense of peace. Let Him do that for you, Cecily and let him direct your path. Let God show you what your next move should be."

Cecily pulled away from her mother, grabbed a napkin and wiped her eyes. Without saying a word, she began clearing the dishes from the dining room table. "I can do that, Cecily," Rhonda offered as she placed a supportive hand on her friends back.

"Thanks, but I need to keep busy while he's here. Got to keep myself occupied so that I don't run in there and try to slit his throat." Cecily continued working away, putting away the leftovers and running dishwater. She was about to start washing dishes when Andrew stepped in the kitchen.

"Thank you, Mama Shirley for letting me see the kids. Cecily, I'll be home later tonight. I hope that we can talk and maybe make a couple of decisions about how to handle things. Bye and Merry Christmas." He turned and walked back out towards the front door. Everyone stood still except Rhonda; she took off and followed him outside.

"Andrew, just so you know, I don't appreciate the fact that you put your hands on me. The only reason I didn't call the cops was to spare Cecily the additional drama, but make no mistake, touch me again and your ass goes to jail. Touch Cecily and your ass goes to..."

Andrew threw up his hand to interrupt her threats. "Rhonda, we've always been cool and I'm sorry about how I handled things last night. But if you remember, you attacked Karen first; I was simply trying to break y'all up."

"No, you were trying to protect that deceptive bitch."

"I'm not going to stand here and listen to you bad mouth her. I have to go and I have every confidence that you'll give Cecily all the support she needs." Andrew got in his car and sped away leaving Rhonda dismayed over what an arrogant jackass he'd become.

CHAPTER 23

Hannah lugged her bags up the stairs, put her key in the lock and swung the door open. As soon as she closed the door behind her, she was stunned and knocked off of her feet by the sharp pain that struck her across the face. She shook her head in an effort to regain her bearings, tried to stand to her feet but was kicked back down. Her mind was flying; clearly there was an intruder in the apartment. Thinking that she would need to identify her attacker, Hannah looked up and was shocked to be staring into the face of her roommate.

Red faced and bleeding from her mouth, Hannah stumbled to her feet. "What in the hell is wrong with you?" She demanded. But Karen remained stoned faced and once again smacked Hannah across the face. Standing there expecting no retaliation, Karen was shocked when Hannah returned a punch just as powerful as the one she'd received. "Karen, I'm not trying to fight you so let that be the last punch that's thrown. We are grown women and shouldn't be fighting like animals. Now clearly you have a problem with me, if you want to talk about it that's fine, but if you touch me again, I'm calling the cops."

In a rage, Karen charged Hannah, grabbed her by the throat and rammed her against the wall. "If you ever think of calling the cops on me I'll have your ass locked back up so quick it'll make your head spin! You hear me?" Karen was gasping for air as she reached for the old, medal stapler that was resting on the desk beside her. Finally reaching it, she raised it high and came down across the side of Karen's head. Karen dropped like a sack of potatoes.

The six minutes it took for Karen to come around seemed like an eternity. Hannah had been holding her in her arms and praying that no real damage had been done. She thanked God above as Karen's eyes fluttered and she started easing up from her involuntary nap. "Are you ok, Karen? Let me help you up."

Looking at Hannah with a whole new respect, Karen scampered away from her. "You stay the hell away from me. I ought to have you thrown back in jail tonight."

"Maybe we should call the cops and both of us take our chances on jail." Hannah suggested. She knew how important Karen's career was to her and how she had high hopes for an upcoming promotion. Karen didn't want the cops involved in this anymore than Hannah did. "Now why did you attack me in the first place?"

"Because I told you I needed you here, told you not to leave, but you left anyway. And the other night Rhonda busted up in here and caught me and Andrew together, now everything is blown to hell. Cecily knows and all of my careful planning was in vain."

"I can't believe that you thought she wouldn't eventually figure it out in the first place. Your dumb ass plan was flawed from the beginning. At least now everything is out in the open, they can just divorce like normal people and you and Andrew can run off into the sunset."

"You are so stupid! Andrew will never leave her; he will not have his children being raised in a broken home. He's always wanted a traditional family for his children and this mess isn't going to change that. You still have a job to do...Cecily has got to die.

CHAPTER 24

Cecily sat on the side of the bed still trying to digest the words that Andrew had shoved down her throat. They were so disrespectful and his demands so outrageous that it all sat in the pit of her stomach like rotten meat, painfully churning and twisting her bowel as she tried to reject them. She had been in this state for two days now, but for the sake of her children, she had to pull herself together. Rachel had actually gone through the pantry, pulled out the bread and peanut butter and made her mom a sandwich in hopes that it would help make her better. The roles had temporarily reversed, the child taking care of the parent and in this case, it was unacceptable.

It didn't take long for Cecily to rip the sheets from her king sized sleigh bed as well as the kids beds and replace them with spring fresh linens. She dusted the bedroom furniture as well as that in the oversized family room, formal living and dining rooms. After vacuuming all of the floors and thoroughly cleaning the kitchen and bathrooms, she was satisfied with the appearance of the house. She climbed the stairs and then stopped as she crossed the bridge that overlooked the downstairs area. The two story family room, the crystal chandelier that hung perfectly in the foyer, the granite counter tops and stainless steel appliances, it was all so beautiful, but not worth the price she was paying to have it. She shook the thoughts from her head and continued down the hall to prepare herself and the children for an afternoon of fun.

"Mama, where are we going?" Brian asked excitedly.

Cecily pulled the car out of the drive and smiled broadly as she replied. "It's a surprise; you guys will have to be patient for just a few more minutes." A co-worker had told her about a place called Andretti's. It was a huge indoor game room housing everything from ski-ball to go-cart racing and she was hoping that the kids would enjoy all it had to offer.

"Mama, we've been riding forever, how much longer before we're there?" Rachel whined.

"Oh please little girl, you've been riding for fifteen minutes and will be at your surprise in another five minutes. So y'all just cool your heels and listen to the music. Cecily turned up the volume to their favorite Kids Bop CD and sang along with the kid friendly version of Cee Lo Green's song "Forget You." Rachel and Brian laughed and begged Cecily to be quiet. It was a running joke in the family that for as much as Cecily liked to sing, she couldn't carry a tune in a bucket. And of course, their cries for silence were encouragement for her to sing even louder. Finally, she pulled into a parking space, turned off the car and giggled as she heard Rachel take a deep sigh and mumble "Thank goodness."

"What is this place, what all is inside there?" Brian inquired as he looked at the large building with pictures of cars painted across it.

"Let's just go in. Your Aunt Rhonda is waiting for us inside and we don't want to keep her waiting." The three of them held hands and walked to the large structure. Rhonda was waiting for them just inside the door and greeted each of them with hugs and kisses. But by now the children realized what type of place they were in and offered only half hearted hugs. It wasn't that they weren't happy to see Rhonda, but they were more excited by all of the bells and whistles of the most amazing playground they'd ever seen. And just when they thought they'd seen it all, Rhonda announced that she already had their tickets for go-cart racing.

"This is so awesome! Mama, can we play all of these games?" Brian continues his barrage of questions.

"You can play as many as fifty dollars can buy. That's twenty-five dollars each, you guys have your own play cards and I'll show you how to swipe them to make the games work." After a quick tutorial, the kids were excitedly playing games, winning tickets to be redeemed for prizes, and competing for bragging rights. As solemn as Cecily had been over the last few days, the pure joy of her kids made her smile from the inside out. But Rhonda could look in her eyes and still see the pain that was lying just below the surface.

"You know, I've known you for a very long time, I see this sadness in you. I'm praying so hard for you, Cecily."

"I need every bit of that prayer. There's so much going on, more than you know. I just don't know what to do, Rhonda. Seems like all of my options lead to a place that I absolutely don't want to go."

"What do you mean by 'more than I know'?"

"Let's just enjoy the kids, have a little fun ourselves and when I drop them off at Mom's for the night, we'll go out and talk."

"Okay, that sounds like a plan. And since our go cart race isn't for another hour, I'm going to grab us a couple of play cards so that we can get in on the action. Be right back."

Three hours and one hundred fifty dollars later, Cecily drove with her sleeping children to her mom's house. As hard as it was for her to get into full function mode this morning, she was glad she did. The kids had an amazing time and experienced their mom as the usual caring, fun loving woman they've always known and that meant everything to her. Cecily desperately wanted the kids to be as unaffected by her problems as possible. Of course they knew that things were different. Their dad was seldom home and mom had been crying, but that had to change. Cecily had no control over Andrew, but she could control the state that the children saw her in. No more would they see her shedding tears over her worthless excuse for a husband. They deserved better and quite frankly, so did she. Andrew wasn't even worth her tears.

ððð

Rhonda was escorted to a nice corner table at the popular Buckhead restaurant Twist. The atmosphere was a little noisy, but she wanted to keep Cecily's spirits up with some good background music and plenty of smiling faces. She knew that Cecily would be arriving any minute and took the liberty of ordering them a couple of Pomegranate Martinis. And just as the drinks arrived, so did Cecily.

"Hey girl, I hope you haven't been waiting too long."

"No, not at all. I've just been here long enough to secure us some starter drinks. So take a couple of sips so you can begin to tell me all the latest news."

Cecily took her friends advice and downed her drink in record time. As soon as the waiter walked by, she ordered another round. "Now that I've had a little something to calm my nerves I can tell you this foolishness that Andrew is talking. You remember how I told you he refuses to have the kids raised in a broken home?" Rhonda nodded her affirmation. "Well, with all he's done and continues to do, he's still sticking with that demand. Says he won't grant me a divorce. If I file, he'll have it tied up in the courts for years."

"So you're supposed to play happy wife while he screws your friend every night?"

"Pretty much. He says that neither of us have been happy for a long time, but we must put the kid's needs ahead of our own. He's promised to be home more often for dinner like he used to be and offered to move into the guest room. He insists that we have to occasionally show one another affection in front of Rachel and Brian. He will hang out with me in our bedroom until they've gone to sleep, then he'll either leave or go to his room. If he leaves, he'll *try* to make it back by the time they wake up for school. Have you ever heard anything so absurd?"

"He sounds like a crazy man," Rhonda asserted. The look on her face was one of pure disbelief.

"He may sound crazy, but he's as serious as a heart attack. Rhonda, I know I haven't been living the most righteous life, but I deserve better than this. I don't know what I'll do yet, how I'll get out of this situation, but I have to find a way. Carter offers me love and respect; I won't continue to put him or my happiness off for the bullshit that Andrew is shoving at me."

CHAPTER 25

Surprisingly, Andrew had decided to come home and spend the night. Lately, most of his weekends were spent elsewhere. Too bad he hadn't announced this ahead of time, Cecily could have informed him that the kids were spending the weekend with her mother. His presence in the house was defeating the point of sending Rachel and Brian away. Cecily had wanted to give her babies a fun filled day, have girl talk with Rhonda and then stay in solitude for the remainder of the weekend. All she could hope for now was that Andrew had no expectations of her. She wanted no conversation from him, wouldn't be cooking for him, didn't even want to smell the scent of his crappy cologne. She wanted him gone.

Andrew went into the kitchen, leaned against the counter and watched as Cecily poured herself a glass of wine. "So tell me again why the kids are with your mother?"

"Because I thought it would give me a chance to have some time alone. Some peace and quiet so that I could think clearly…alone."

"Will you pour me a glass of that?"

Cecily placed a beautiful glass cork in the bottle, picked up her wine, and walked away. She ascended the stairs and closed herself in the bedroom. After taking a big gulp from her glass, she picked up a stack of DVD's and began shuffling through them. It didn't take long to decide on *V For Vendetta*, it had become one of her favorites. She changed into her comfy PJ's, popped in the movie and relaxed across the California King. The movie was powerful, touching, and a welcome distraction. Then without warning, the bedroom door swung open and in walked Andrew. Instantly her relaxed mood became tense and guarded. What in the hell could he want? "What is it, Andrew?"

"It's lonely out there," He teased. "What are you watching and do you mind if I join you?"

Cecily sighed deeply, making her irritation very apparent. "I'm watching *V For Vendetta* and yes, I do mind. Again, it is my intention to spend tonight and the remainder of the weekend alone."

"You're not picking the kids up tomorrow?"

"No Andrew, if you want to see them you'll have to do so over at Mom's place. She has already planned out their weekend and I'm not going to pull them away from that. I would suggest you call Mom first to make sure that they'll be home."

"I wish you had consulted with me before sending them off."

"And I wish you had not cheated with my best friend. But it just goes to show that we can't all have what we want."

"Fine, I'll leave you alone because I don't even want to start that argument again." Andrew turned around and walked out closing the door behind him. It wasn't long before he jumped in his car and left for the night. Cecily breathed a sigh of relief as she heard the car garage open and close. She rewound her movie to where it was before her interruption and relaxed into the bed. As exhaustion began to take over, Cecily struggled to stay awake until the end of the movie. Once it ended, she tuned into the soft jazz music channel. It provided the light sounds that would lull her to sleep. Just as she drifted off, she heard her phone chime. It was text message from Carter wanting to know if she could talk. As if someone injected her with a shot of adrenaline, she was wide awake, letting him know that it was safe to call.

"Hi there, love." There seemed to be a sweet, gentle excitement to Carter's voice that made Cecily feel warm and cared for.

"Hi, how are you? How was your day?"

"It was pretty busy, the office was swamped today. I thought I'd never get through drawing and processing blood. If I never hear the word venipuncture again it'll be fine with me. But I didn't call to talk about work; I called to hear your beautiful voice. How has your day been?"

"It was pretty good until a couple of hours ago. The kids and I had a great time at that game room. We especially loved the go cart racing, it was a blast."

"Well what happened a couple of hours ago to ruin the rest of your day?"

"I had an unexpected house companion. I dropped the kids off at my mom's for the remainder of the weekend and then tonight their father shows up. Fortunately, he accepted that I didn't want to be bothered and left."

"Don't be annoyed with me, but out of everything you just said all I heard was that you were alone for the weekend."

Cecily couldn't refrain from laughing. "Yes, I am alone this weekend, but I don't understand why that's all you heard."

"Because it means that there is a possibility of you spending a significant amount of time with me over the next couple of days. What do you think? Is that a strong possibility?"

"Absolutely! I would love nothing more than to share time and space with you. What did you have in mind?"

"Why don't you come over tomorrow and we'll just play it by ear? Oh, and since you don't have mommy duty, bring clothes and let's make a night of it. I may even throw in breakfast Sunday morning."

"I don't know how safe that breakfast thing is, but I'm willing to take a chance. I'll see you tomorrow." As Cecily spoke, it was easy to hear the joy in her voice. There was no denying that this man made her happy, it was a blissful fact.

"Okay then, you sleep well and I'll see you soon. Nitey night."

"Goodnight."

ððð

"Good morning, Mom, how are you guys doing? Are the kids behaving for you?"

"Of course they are, my grandbabies are so sweet and never give me a minutes trouble."

"Don't you think that's a slight exaggeration?" Cecily asked with a chuckle.

"No! Now moving on, how did you enjoy your night of peace and quiet? I hope you took full advantage of it and got some rest."

Cecily hit the speaker button on the phone and placed it on the vanity so that she could continue her conversation while combing her hair and applying her makeup. "It was a good evening for the most part. There was a little hiccup when Andrew decided to show up. He wanted to pretend as if all was well between us. Even wanted to crawl into bed and watch a movie with me."

"You have got to be kidding?"

"Sadly, I'm not. But I remained calm and stressed to him that it was my desire to be alone. It wasn't too long before he grabbed his keys and left."

"Well I'm glad that there was no type of confrontation. Now moving on, what are your plans for the day? I'm going to take the kids to the aquarium and wasn't sure if you'd be joining us for a while or what."

"Mom I think I'm going to let you guys enjoy that without me. I have some errands to run and a little shopping to do. But I'll call you later so that the kids can tell me all about their day."

"Alright then, I'll talk to you later. And remember, I love you."

"I love you too, Mom."

Forty-five minutes later Cecily was browsing the racks of Dillard's lingerie department. She wanted to get something sexy and sophisticated. Something that would caress her body and feel good to Carter's touch. A look of satisfaction settled on her face as she reached for the perfect negligee. As she made her way to the register, she realized how frivolous it was to be spending money on more lingerie when she already had so much. But if it got her the kind of reaction she was hoping for, then it would be money well spent. With her package in hand Cecily moved on to her next stop, the MAC cosmetics counter in Macy's. She had been out of her favorite lip gloss for a week. A few more stops and a quick lunch in the mall food court brought Cecily's shopping journey to an end. She returned home to relax a while before preparing to head out for the night.

CHAPTER 26

Carter stood handsome and tall in his trademark grey and black sweats waiting to greet his overnight guest. Cecily killed the ignition and unlocked the doors. As soon as she stepped out of her car, Carter wrapped her in his warm embrace. The hold they had on one another was full of emotion. Cecily melted into Carter and felt as if she was exactly where she was supposed to be…home. Finally releasing each other, Carter retrieved her bag from the backseat of the car and escorted her into his sanctuary.

"So what are we doing this evening, Mr. Everton?" Cecily quizzed as she snuggled into the corner of his couch.

"I found this nice little spot that features great local jazz artists. A little music, a bite to eat, and then see where the night takes us. How does that sound?"

"It sounds really nice. Now how long will I have to wait for you to get ready?"

Carter cocked his head to the side and gave a little smirk. "Give me ten minutes and I'll be ready to rock and roll." That said, he disappeared around the corner and into the bathroom for a quick shower. Twenty-five minutes later, Carter emerged dressed and ready to go.

Sweet Georgia's Juke Joint did not disappoint. Cecily loved the ambiance and the music was fantastic. Sadly she didn't get to partake of the menu options that sounded the most delectable. Instead she settled for a tasty salad, but it was still just a salad. Carter questioned her as to why she was eating so light. Cecily told a little white lie stating that she just wasn't that hungry. Truth be told, she didn't want to look or feel all bloated when they returned home for the more intimate part of their night. But Carter didn't need to know that, all he needed to know was that she was thrilled to be with him. They held hands, talked, and flirted like a couple of teenage kids.

As soon as Carter closed the door to his place, he walked up behind Cecily, removed her coat and took her purse. Before she could move an inch, he stepped to her and began to seductively kiss her on the neck. Traveling between her neck and her mouth, each kiss became more passionate than the last. His hands caressed her face; slowly they moved down and began to remove her blouse. Cecily didn't even remember how it happened, but before she knew it she was standing completely naked in this man's living room and he was on his knees enjoying the taste of her womanly juices. Cecily stood there in sheer ecstasy. Rising to his feet, Carter turned Cecily around, bent her over the back of his couch and took her from behind. Not having ever experienced anything like this, her mind was completely blown. Just when she thought it couldn't get any better, he stood her up and walked her into the kitchen. Carter lifted and sat her on the counter top. Raising her legs, he once again feasted on her sweet nectar. Just as he entered her again, Cecily heard herself whimper, "What are you doing to me?"

With her legs now wrapped around his body, he carried her to the couch and laid her down. Their moans and groans of passion filled the room until both had reached the most amazing orgasms of their lives. Cecily was completely and utterly satisfied. If she never had sex again it would be okay because she realized that she'd just experienced the greatest seduction of all time.

CHAPTER 27

Karen paced the floor, her mind flying as she tried to figure out how she could get Andrew to leave Cecily. She'd decided that if there was another alternative to having Cecily knocked off she'd take it. After all, Cecily had been an amazing friend to her. It was Cecily that loaned her money when she was flat broke. It was Cecily standing by her side and holding her hand as she went through the pain of her divorce. Yes, she had indeed been a good friend, but it was time for her life with Andrew to end. Karen felt as if her friend never really appreciated her husband and it was now time to pass him to someone that would love everything about him.

"Why are you looking so intense?" Hannah quizzed as she emerged from her bedroom still dressed in pajamas.

Karen shot her the evil eye as if to scold her for speaking without having been spoken to first. Without a word, Karen returned to her pacing and strategizing.

"If you walk a hole in the carpet we'll lose our security deposit. I don't know about you, but when I move out I want to take as much money as I can with me." Hannah stood a couple of feet away with her neck crooked and looking at her roommate with a sarcastic smirk. "And sadly, your intense look has morphed into one of severe constipation. You better relax before you have an accident on yourself."

Stopping in her tracks, Karen shot Hannah with a million invisible daggers. "I think I've had just about enough of your smart ass mouth. If you can't come out here and talk like you have some damn sense then I suggest you don't talk at all."

"Be careful now, you're starting to sound an awful lot like a mom. Fortunately not my mom, but a mom none-the-less. All you need to do is wag a finger the next time you say something like that." Hannah was truly enjoying harassing Karen and the look on Karen's face let her know that she was doing a great job. But then she could see the light bulb go on over Karen's head. What ridiculous idea could have popped into that deranged head of hers?

"You're right; I do sound like a mother." Her expression delivered the message that she'd just been hit with the best idea ever. "I can't believe I didn't think of this way before now. Sometimes your smart ass mouth can actually deliver a good idea. Andrew doesn't want any of his children to come from a broken home, it stands to reason that that would apply to any kids that I have with him as well. He can't stand that damn Cecily, but he loves me. If I have his child, he would willingly leave her and build a new life with me and our child. We could get custody of Rachel and Brian and all live as one big happy family." Karen was overjoyed with her revelation. Then she noticed the expression on Hannah's face. "Why are you looking at me like that?" Karen demanded.

"Because you sound like a stark raving lunatic." Hannah shook her head in disgust and continued her journey into the kitchen. After taking only three steps she could feel Karen breathing down her neck, following her step for step. Hannah stopped abruptly. "Why are you all up behind me? You need to back up and give me some space."

"Don't you ever call me crazy! I am not a lunatic nor do I sound like one. Never make the mistake of calling me crazy again, understand?"

"I understand you need to step out of my personal space. I also understand that if you don't want to be called crazy, then you need to stop behaving like you are. Now move."

Karen walked around Hannah and took a seat on one of the kitchen chairs. "You are in need of a reality check and I'm such a nice person that I'm going to give you one right now. The reality is that I have the power to send your ass back to prison with a simple phone call. You are in violation of your parole and if you don't control your tongue, I'll make sure that Big Bertha on cell block twelve controls it for you." Without speaking a word, Hannah turned and left the room. "Cat got your tongue now?" There was no reply from Hannah. Karen snickered like some juvenile delinquent. "I knew that would shut your smart mouth up."

Just as she was passing through the living room, the doorbell rang. Hannah detoured from her original path to see who wanted to enter what she considered her hell hole. "Hi Andrew, come on in." Andrew stepped into the apartment and planted his usual kiss on Hannah's cheek.

"How are you today young lady?"

"I was in a really good mood. Sadly, it didn't last as long as I'd hoped it would." Hannah confessed as she cut her eyes over at Karen. Her annoyance didn't go unnoticed by Andrew.

"Well darling you need to recapture that good mood. You can't allow people, things, or situations to steal away your happiness."

Placing her hand on her hip and cocking her head towards Karen she responded, "Sometimes that easier said than done. Especially when you're dealing directly with the devil." She didn't wait to hear what foolishness would escape Karen's mouth. She turned on her heels and went to her room. She decided that the best thing she could do for herself was get dressed and get the hell out of that apartment.

Half an hour later she emerged from her bedroom fully dressed and keys in hand. She could hear Andrew and Karen's moans and groans penetrating through the door that separated them from the rest of the house and it was enough to make her want to throw up. Luckily her cell phone rang before nausea completely took over. She dug it out of her purse and saw that it was Rhonda calling. Suddenly she felt sick all over again. "Hello."

"Hi Hannah, this is Rhonda. How are you today?"

"Hey…I'm doing well, and you?"

"I'll be doing a lot better if you'll agree to meet me for lunch. I know that you don't want to be in the middle of this mess with Karen, Andrew, and Cecily, but I have a couple of questions and would really appreciate just ten minutes. How about it?"

Against her better judgment, Hannah agreed to meet Rhonda at the Five Guy's burger joint midway between their homes. She purposely arrived ten minutes early so that she could have time to collect her thoughts and relax her nerves before Rhonda showed up. But as soon as Rhonda walked through the door, Hannah's heart began to race. Rhonda was not alone; Cecily was walking in beside her and Hannah felt like she'd been set up.

"Relax, Hannah, I promise I didn't come here looking for a fight." Cecily reassured her with a light touch on her shoulder. "And please don't blame Rhonda, I asked her not to mention my coming along because I was afraid you'd say no. Is it okay if we sit down?"

Hannah nodded her approval as she nervously cracked open the free peanuts that adorned the table. She glanced at Rhonda who was clearly trying to avert her eyes away from Hannah. The two of them had talked briefly since the holidays, but Hannah was very clear about her objection to being caught in the middle of Andrew, Karen, and Cecily's triangle. Yet here she was smack dab in the middle of it all. She could only imagine the barrage of questions that she was about to be hit with. "Cecily, I'm sure you have a million questions, but I don't know that I'm the one to answer them. You have to realize that it is not my desire to be in the midst of all the mess that's going on and honestly, I thought that Rhonda here would have conveyed that to you."

"I know you aren't pleased with the way I did this, Hannah, but please put yourself in Cecily's shoes for just a moment. I mean really, her husband is screwing her best friend and is refusing to divorce her. She needs as much information as she can get so that she can fight this man in court for her freedom and for her kids." Rhonda pleaded her friend's case hoping that her words weren't falling on deaf ears.

Cecily's mind was flying trying to figure out what she could do or say to get Hannah to open up to her. All the time, Hannah was thinking of the ridiculous plans that Karen had plotted and how she absolutely could not speak of either of them. As much as she wanted to help Cecily, she could not, would not risk her own freedom to do so. "How about I go and grab us some burgers and fries and we just share a meal and see where the conversation leads us?" Cecily tried to sound casual but her eyes were pleading for Hannah to say yes. And again, against her better judgment, Hannah did agree. She and Rhonda sat silently while Cecily went to place their food order. "I didn't know what kind of soda y'all wanted so I just brought you the cups and you can go fill up on whatever soda you prefer."

They consumed their food with only small spurts of conversation that mainly centered around the weather. But Hannah found that the longer she sat there, the more small talk they made, the more compassion she began to have for Cecily. "Cecily, I can't promise that I can answer all of your questions, but I will answer what I can."

Cecily didn't waste any time, she jumped right in before Hannah could change her mind. "How long have they been seeing one another?"

"For quite some time now. I'm not exactly sure of how long because they were already dating when I moved in with Karen."

Cecily shook her head in disbelief but continued on with her questions. "Did you know from the beginning that he was married?"

"I never saw a wedding band on his hand so it never really occurred to me to ask if he was married or not." Hannah now realized what a mistake it was to allow Cecily to ask her anything. She didn't want to lie but really had no choice. "You remember the little confrontation that followed our initial introduction? Well it was after that incident that Karen broke down and told me the truth."

"How often is he over at her apartment?"

"Cecily, I think it was a mistake to let you ask me all these questions. I really need to continue my living situation with Karen and this will only jeopardize it."

"Hannah, I swear I won't let her know that you shared anything with me. Please, just two more questions?"

Hannah reluctantly agreed to just two more questions. "Go ahead, Cecily, but seriously this is it. I don't want to be caught up in all of this." Hannah heard the words coming out of her mouth, but what she actually wanted to say, wanted to scream was Karen's plan to get her away from Andrew. She wanted to tell Cecily that she could save herself a lot of pain and possibly her life by simply divorcing Andrew. Staying married to that dog was not worth her life.

"He's hardly ever at home anymore; I just want to know if he's spending all that time with Karen?"

"He's there two to three nights a week. He keeps clothes in her closet and grooming products in her bathroom."

Cecily began blinking rapidly, a poor attempt to keep the multitude of tears that were stinging her eyes from falling down her face. "Has Karen said what she thinks their affair will lead to?"

"Marriage." Hannah responded very matter-of-factly. She stood to her feet, grabbed her purse, and placed a sympathetic hand on Cecily's shoulder. "I'm sorry." Hannah left the restaurant scared to death that she'd just signed the papers that would send her back to prison.

Cecily remained at the table and the tears that once threatened to fall had found their escape and ran freely down her face. "You know the funny thing is, I'm no longer upset with Andrew. We've been broken for a long time now. My anger and hurt are a product of Karen's unbelievable betrayal. And if she thinks for two seconds that Andrew is going to marry her, she's a bigger fool than I thought."

CHAPTER 28

Rhonda drove through the city thinking of all that was wrong in Cecily's life. She had learned to cope with the idea of having a chronic illness and with the help of Dr. Douglas, she was managing the effects of her sickle cell pretty well. But what she found unbearable, unacceptable, and just plain old painful was her love life. Looking at Cecily's situation made Rhonda more determined than ever to not fall in love. She'd decided a while back not to allow herself to become vulnerable to any man. It simply wasn't worth the heartache.

One thing that Rhonda wasn't willing to deny herself was the basic need for companionship and physical contact. She'd met Roy seven months ago. He was an average looking man of average height and weight, but his smile and personality made him pretty close to phenomenal. They had met at a networking event that Rhonda attended on behalf of her company. She was standing with a small group of executives chatting about the state of the economy when Roy walked up and joined the conversation. That day marked the beginning of their involvement.

Roy had been a patient man. He and Rhonda had talked and consistently gone out for three months before she allowed him to kiss her and it was another two months before things became physical. Once they did cross that line, Rhonda was tickled pink that he was close to phenomenal in bed as well. But what she didn't like was that he was constantly professing his love for her. Everything that Rhonda had ever observed about relationships told her that love complicated things.

Her parents seemed like the perfect couple, all of the other neighborhood couples were jealous of their love. What they didn't see were the arguments over the imaginary men that her dad accused her mom of flirting with. His love drove him to insane heights of jealousy and obsessive behavior and it drained damn near every bit of happiness right out of her mom. Rhonda had also witnessed Karen's ex-husband use her love for him as a weapon against her. He knew how Karen adored him and he took her love, adoration, money, and self-respect. What he gave her in return was a STD and a "Dear John" letter that explained his reasons for leaving. *"Dear Karen, you love me too much and if I stay I will only cause you pain because I can't return that love. Take care, Paul."* Karen was devastated and her current actions made Rhonda question whether or not she was acting out as a means of coping with her pain. No...love wasn't in the cards for Rhonda, the cost of it was just too damn high.

Maneuvering through the city, Rhonda found herself getting excited about her evening. She fought hard to keep her feelings intact, but couldn't deny how much fun she always had with Roy. Tonight they were going out to dinner and meeting some of Roy's friends at the bowling alley. Rhonda hadn't bowled in years and prayed that she wouldn't make a complete fool of herself. The loud ringing of her phone pulsating through the car speakers startled her, interrupting her train of thought. "Hello."

"Hey, cutie pie, wanted to let you know that I got held up here at work so I'll be picking you up a little bit later than planned."

"How much later?"

"I'll only be delayed by about thirty minutes. Is that okay with you?"

"That'll be fine. I haven't even made it home myself so this gives me a little breathing room. I'll see you when you get to the house."

"Perfect! I'll see you soon and Rhonda…I love you." Roy immediately hung up the phone; he didn't want to wait on the line while Rhonda fished for something to say in return.

Bowling had turned out better than Rhonda had predicted. Until now, she'd only met one of Roy's friends and was a little nervous about meeting all of his closest buddies. To her pleasant surprise, everyone was kind and very welcoming. Even her bowling game was better than she'd expected it be, a score of 175 wasn't half bad. Roy drove his date back home and as always, he was thrilled to be invited into the house for a night cap. One thing led to another and midnight found the couple snuggled up in bed basking in the afterglow. "Baby, you're an incredible woman, everyone thought you were the best thing since sliced bread and that we made a cute couple."

"I must admit, I had a great time and everyone was just as sweet as they could be."

"So when do I get to meet some of your friends?"

Rhonda pulled away putting a little space between the two of them. "Babe, you know how much I enjoy our time, but if I start introducing you to everyone they are going to immediately start pestering me about marriage, if I think that you're the one, and all that jazz. I just don't think I'm ready for that."

"Are you sure that's it or are you worried that they won't accept you being in a relationship with a white dude?"

"Oh please, my friends are no more racist than I am and I wish you wouldn't say such foolish things."

"Seven months and I haven't met a soul. Surely you can see how this makes me a little concerned? I just want to know that I'm as important to you as you are to me."

"You are, Roy. There's no way I could spend this much time with you and be intimate with you like this and not care for you. But I understand your concern and I promise it'll be soon. You'll meet everyone closest to me very soon." She reassured him by snuggling back up to him and planting gentle kisses on his chest. And the more she snuggled with him the more turned on she became. The visual of her dark chocolate skin poured across his pale tones was more of an aphrodisiac than she wanted to admit. As for Roy, he had heard all of these promises before, but with Rhonda touching him the way that she was, he decided to save the argument for another time. Right now, it was time for round two.

CHAPTER 29

The kids took off running through the house as soon as Cecily opened the door. She followed behind and carelessly tossed her briefcase onto the kitchen counter. Cecily kicked her shoes off right there in the kitchen and began to peruse the refrigerator for what she could prepare for dinner. She knew that she had to go ahead and get it done because if she went to her room first or sat on the couch, they would be having dinner delivered again. While Chinese delivery was convenient for her, it wasn't a nutritionally sound option for the kids. It didn't take long to settle on chicken and pasta Alfredo, Caesar salad, and garlic bread. Of course when she started to set the table, Andrew came strolling in like he was still a relevant part of the family.

"Ooh, something smells delicious, what are we having?"

"The kids and I are having Italian; I assumed that you'd be having Karen."

"I see you've got jokes today. Why can't you just be glad that I'm home and ready to spend quality time with my family? Don't you realize that this is what thousands of women long for? You've got a beautiful home, the bills are paid, our kids are healthy, happy, and thriving. What more could you possibly want?"

"You sound like a new fool! An old fool would know better than to even fix his mouth to say some mess like that. I'm not some desperate little girl seeking the love that she was denied by her father. I'm a grown ass woman and I know my worth."

"Daddy, you're home!" Brian rejoiced as he entered the kitchen. Are you going to stay the whole night or do you have to stay at work all night again?"

Andrew lifted his son and wrapped him up in a bear hug. "Daddy is home for the night and if you like, I can take you and your sister to school in the morning."

"Yeah, that would be great." Brian squirmed from his father's arms and took off running. He was excited to share the good news with his sister. A couple of minutes later Rachel made her way into the kitchen with her brother following closely on her heels. "Daddy, Rachel said that she didn't want you to take her to school."

"Baby girl, are you going to come and give your old dad a hug?"

Rachel walked over to Andrew, gave him a half-hearted hug, and then turned her attention to her mother. "Mom, I'm hungry, how much longer before we can eat?"

"Dinner is ready now. Why don't you guys go wash your hands and meet me back at the table?"

Andrew stood there and watched the interaction between mother and daughter and wondered why Rachel hadn't responded to him very positively. He started to ask

Cecily but decided to wait and observe how the rest of the evening went first. He enjoyed every bite of his dinner just as he always did when Cecily cooked. He sat back and watched as the kids placed their empty plates and cups in the sink and ran off to take their baths. Cecily moved about the kitchen, cleaning the counters, washing the dishes, and sweeping the floor. Andrew never offered to lift a finger. Instead, he found himself getting aroused at the site of Cecily working around him. He couldn't deny that she was a beautiful woman with a great body. He still desired her and if all went his way, he'd have her tonight. After all, they were still married and it was her wifely duty to perform for her man.

"Mom, can we stay up just for one more hour? The Power Puff Girl movie is coming on and I really want to see it." Rachel pleaded with her eyes, hoping that her mom would break her 8:00pm bedtime rule.

"I'm sorry honey, but you know the rules. If you stay up you'll be completely exhausted in the morning and I'll catch the devil trying to get you guys up."

"Oh come on." Andrew chimed in. "I think we can break the rule just this one night. You can stay up another hour, baby girl."

"That's okay, Mom said no so I'll go to bed." Rachel turned and left the room without even looking at her father.

An hour later, the kids had been tucked into bed, their school clothes had been ironed, and Cecily had retired to her bedroom. She flipped the television on, lazily moved to the bath, and turned on the hot water in preparation for a relaxing shower. Unfortunately, just as she disrobed and stepped under the water, Andrew walked in lurking at her with a familiar twinkle in his eye. Cecily could only surmise that he'd lost his mind. The fact that Andrew was watching her, trying to hold a conversation with her as she bathed made her incredibly uncomfortable. They were not the couple they used to be and her nakedness was something that she didn't want Andrew observing. As soon as she turned off the water, Cecily wrapped herself in a towel and tried to close the door to the bathroom, but Andrew stuck his foot out denying Cecily her privacy. Refusing to acknowledge Andrew's behavior, Cecily hurried and dressed and tried to breeze past the man that had become a thorn in her side.

"You look beautiful, Cecily. It's been a long time since we've made love and with your appetite for sex, I know you're about to climb the walls." Andrew grabbed his wife's arm and attempted to pull her into an embrace, but Cecily wasn't hearing it.

"Let me go, Andrew. I'm tired and want to go to sleep."

"You look so stressed, let me help you relieve some of that stress, put you in a better place, make you feel good like only I can."

Cecily laughed in his face. He had no idea that she had a man that truly knew how to make her feel like a woman. Carter's good love relieved her of all stress and anxiety. One touch from him sent her straight to the moon. "I'd rather tense up into a tight ball of insanity instead of have you touch me. You've made your choice, it's time you accept that I am no longer an option for your physical release." Cecily climbed into bed, switched off the light, pretended Andrew wasn't there and drifted off to sleep. But twenty minutes later she was awakened by Andrew groping her body and trying to force himself between her legs. Cecily immediately started fighting and clawing away at his face. She managed to raise her leg and knee him in the groin.

"You're going to rape me now, Andrew? This is what you've turned into, a crazed rapist that attacks under the cover of darkness?" Cecily screamed as she rolled out of bed and hit the floor. She scrambled to her feet as Andrew continued to roll around on the bed in agony. "You're a sick bastard and I want to be done with you. I don't give a damn what you say, I want my damn divorce you son-of-a bitch!" Cecily took off down the hall to Rachel's room and climbed in bed with her little girl. It was the one place in the house she knew she'd be able to get some sleep without fear of being attacked.

Andrew watched as Cecily prepared breakfast for the kids and got them ready to leave for school. His anger with her was bubbling just beneath the surface. In that moment he wanted more than anything to snatch Cecily up and slap all hell out of her. But none of that was an option with his kids around. Finally, everyone was ready to leave for school and work. "Alright kids, go jump in the car and I'll be out in a second." Andrew instructed. Once they were safely out of the house, Andrew walked up on Cecily, tightly wrapping his hand around her slender neck.

"Bitch, the last thing you're going to get from me is a divorce. And I don't know what you've told my daughter about me, but you better correct it. I won't have her walking around here ignoring me." He squeezed a little tighter making Cecily eyes bulge out of her head. Seconds later he let her go and she collapsed into a heap on the floor.

CHAPTER 30

Karen walked away from the open door allowing Andrew to enter the apartment. Normally Andrew would have used his key to gain entrance, but when 1:00am rolled around and Karen realized he wasn't coming over, she put the top lock and chain on for security. She hated the idea of him spending the night with Cecily. The very thought of him touching her, kissing her, making love to her made Karen nauseous. In her mind, Andrew belonged to her and no part of him should ever touch another woman, not even his wife.

"So why did you lock me out? You never put all the extra locks on the door."

"After realizing that you weren't coming over, despite the fact that you said you were, I figured I'd better take the extra safety precautions. It's not like there was a man here to protect me in case something happened."

"Baby, I came here to relax and spend a little quality time with you. I'm not up for any of this female drama crap."

"Andrew, you breeze in here whenever you want to and I'm always here to do whatever it takes to make you happy. Now I'm going to need more from you. I sat here in great expectation of your arrival, but you chose to spend the night with that woman. Do you really think that after spending the night alone, knowing that you were over there screwing her, that I'm going to be jumping up and down because you walked in the door offering me your leftovers?"

"I've never offered you leftovers and I wasn't screwing anybody. That bitch wouldn't even sleep in the same room with me!" Andrew spewed his anger.

"Damn it, Andrew, the only reason you didn't have sex with Cecily is because she wouldn't let you. Don't you get it? I'm here offering you everything I've got, but you're not satisfied with that. You want me and her and I'm telling you now, you can't have both. Not to mention the fact that she doesn't even want your ass!"

Without warning, Andrew smacked Karen across the face and she fell back into the wall. She didn't attempt to fight him back, but instead stood there whimpering like a wounded puppy. "Baby, I'm sorry…please forgive me. I let my frustration get the best of me. I certainly didn't mean to take it out on you." Andrew stepped forward and reached out for his lover. He expected for her to reject his weak apology, but instead she allowed him to pull her into his embrace.

"I'm not your punching bag, Andrew. I won't allow you to ever hit me again, I deserve better," Karen declared.

"Yes you do." Lifting her face to meet his, Andrew kissed Karen softly. "I won't put my hands on you again in anger." He kissed her again and again, the kisses becoming more passionate. He ignored the tears that dampened her face and began to disrobe her. In what seemed like a matter of seconds, Karen's clothes were in a pile on the floor and Andrew had her pinned against the wall, aggressively shoving his manhood deeper and deeper into her womb. He may not have been hitting her, but there was no doubt that he was still abusing her and sadly, out of desperation to have him, she allowed the abuse.

Hannah came home to find Karen in the kitchen preparing food for the man that she fantasized would one day be all hers. Andrew sat across the room, reading the paper like he was really the man of the house. It sickened Hannah to see them playing house as if there was nothing wrong with what they were doing. As physically attractive as she found Andrew, Hannah was equally turned off by his lack of loyalty and respect for his family. She'd hoped that they wouldn't notice her creeping past the kitchen, but no such luck.

"Hannah, wow girl, you're looking damn good today. How are you?"

"Thanks, Andrew, I'm doing well. How are you?"

"I bet you do it well, alright." Feeling Karen's eyes burning a hole through him, Andrew decided to curb his flirting a little bit. "I mean I'm glad you're doing well. Karen's making a little brunch, would you like to join us?"

"No thank you, I'm just running in to pick something up. I've got to head right back out." Hannah barely slowed down long enough for the brief exchange of words. She disappeared into her room, grabbed some paperwork, and headed right back out. "It was good seeing you, Andrew." She lied. "I'll see you later, Karen. Y'all take care."

Like some kind of dutiful wife, Karen placed a large plate of food on the table in front of Andrew. "Honey, do you want a cup of coffee with that or just the orange juice?"

"I'll take some coffee with two sugars and a little cream." Andrew tilted his head to the side and watched Karen run about the room fetching him things like she was a well trained pet. He knew that she was desperate to have him, but wondered just how far she was willing to go to make him happy. Without much persuasion, he'd gotten her to perform every perverted sex act that he'd ever fantasized about. He had her waiting on him hand and foot and knew that he could treat her like garbage and she'd still be there offering him her love. A woman this weak could never win his heart, but he was more than happy to let her keep trying. And seeing Hannah, how good she looked, had him wondering if he could push the envelope just a little further with Karen and get her to agree to make one last fantasy come true. "This is delicious! You are one hell of a cook."

One compliment from Andrew and she smiled as if she'd just won the Academy Award. "I'm so glad that you like it. You know, if we were to get married, I would cook like this for you every day."

"What else would you do for me?" Andrew asked seductively.

"Baby, you know that I'd do anything for you. I'd never make you beg for sex the way that Cecily does. It would be my job to please you in every way possible."

"Are you sure about that? You'd do anything?"

"Anything," Karen promised as she licked her lips.

"I'd like to bring someone else into the bed with us. Another woman. Can you imagine how hot that would be? I can't think of a bigger turn on than to see you kissing and touching another woman and to then join the two of you. I'm getting excited just thinking about it."

In that moment Karen could've been knocked off of her feet with a feather. This was not the direction she wanted this conversation to go in. She was trying to lead him down the path of marriage and he was leading her down the path of perversion. How had things gotten so far off track? "Am I not enough for you?"

"Of course you are enough for me. You're a phenomenal woman and an excellent lover. I just thought that a little extra spice would maybe take us up to that next level of intimacy, that's all." Andrew knew that his play on words could close the deal for him.

"I'm not sure that this would lead us to higher heights or pull you away from me, Andrew. I want us to share a closeness that no one or nothing can touch. I'm not convinced that bringing in someone else won't separate you from me. I can't be sure that your love and affection won't turn a cold shoulder to me. I'm not strong enough to always be concerned about you seeing this new woman without me…behind my back. I don't think that I can handle it." Karen plopped down in the chair feeling weary from Andrew's request. She was trying so hard to be all the woman that he needed, the woman that Cecily hadn't been able to be. Still, it wasn't enough. Tears filled her eyes as doubt filled her heart.

Andrew lovingly placed his hand on Karen's. "Baby, I didn't mean to make you cry. This was only a suggestion and if you're not cool with it then that's okay. I don't want you doing anything that you're not comfortable with. Don't worry about me being taken away by another woman; it's simply not going to happen. I'm with you and with you is exactly where I want to be." Leaning in, he kissed her cheek and wiped her tears.

Karen's head was spinning. How could she not do everything within her power to make this man happy? Surely not meeting his needs and not being secure in their love is what caused him to stray from Cecily. She had to be a better woman. "Who did you have in mind, Andrew?"

He causally lifted his eyes and calmly said, "Hannah."

CHAPTER 31

Floating on cloud nine, Cecily finished over packing for her weekend getaway. She'd already dropped the kids off at her mom's house and they were not sad to see her go. They were excited about their own travel plans to Savannah, Georgia. But their level of excitement still wasn't enough to eclipse Cecily's. Two days alone with Carter was going to be like a dream come true. They'd had the opportunity to spend a rare night alone here and there, but this weekend would allow them the opportunity to talk, laugh and love without the worry of time constraints. She checked her watch and realized that if she didn't leave immediately she'd never make it to Carter's house on time. They had a scheduled departure time of 8:00am and she'd planned to stick to it.

Forty minutes later and fifteen minutes late, Cecily whipped into Carter's subdivision. She approached his townhome but was a bit confused when she didn't see his car waiting outside. He'd advised her that he was packed and that the car was loaded and waiting out front. Timidly she approached the front door, but he flung it open before she could even reach for the doorbell. The smile on his face spoke volumes, he was just as thrilled as she was to be escaping the area with his lady love.

"Sweets, where's the car, I thought you were all packed and ready to go?" Cecily asked as she enjoyed their long embrace hello.

"I am ready, love." Carter pulled away, set the alarm and locked the door. He took Cecily by the hand and led her to the bad ass black convertible Camaro parked across the street. "I figured we'd thoroughly enjoy the weather and let the wind blow through our hair." Carter chuckled.

"I love it!" Cecily giggled like a little kid as they shoved her bags into the small trunk and back seat. The sound of the engine purring was part of the perfect sound track that would accompany them to Gatlinburg, Tennessee. They talked, laughed, listened to music, and took pictures along the way. But for Carter, the loveliest view was that of Cecily sitting beside him with the wind tousling her hair. She seemed so happy and that brought him an enormous amount of joy.

Cecily was hoping against all hope that Carter was as overjoyed as she was. She watched him drive, listened to him talk, and marveled at how incredibly handsome he was. They stopped for gas and as he walked back out of the convenience store, she was struck by how much he reminded her of a modern day James Dean. So smooth, sexy, cool.

The weekend could not have gone better. During the day they wondered around the quaint little town, soaking up the sights, they even got a little daring and went zip lining through the Smokey Mountains. The evenings, they traveled over to Pigeon Forge to enjoy the festivities of the main strip. They played like kids in the arcade and drove like maniacs on the go-cart course. The nights found them in the deluxe suite of the Park Vista making love as if they'd never get the chance again. It was perfect.

ððð

The reality of being back in Atlanta hit Cecily harder than she ever expected. It hadn't been a good thirty minutes since she'd left Carter's home and her decision to stop at a local Wal-Mart would prove to be a bad one. She hadn't seen Karen since learning of the affair she was having with Andrew. But that ended the moment that she aimlessly bumped her cart into someone else's. She looked up to offer an apology and found herself looking in the eyes of her now mortal enemy.

"Cecily, it's been a while. How are you doing?"

"Seriously…you're asking me how I am like we're still cool and everything is everything? Are you crazy?"

"Look, I don't want to fight with you. I know that things have changed and you may be a little hurt by the turn of events with me and Andrew. But I also know that you realize how unhappy he's been in your marriage. This could really be a great thing for all involved. You haven't been happy either and this may very well be your golden opportunity to get out of a bad marriage. You get your freedom and I get my man."

"Bitch, you have really lost your mind!" Cecily exclaimed a little louder than she intended to. "My marriage is none of your concern; my husband should never have even been a blip on your radar. You were supposed to be my friend; I have done more shit for you and been there for you more than anyone else in your sorry ass life. And this is how you repay me?"

"Oh please, the only reason you've ever done anything for me is so that you could run back and brag about what a helpful, thoughtful friend you are. It's never been about lifting me up; it's always been about you getting recognized for your good deeds. Even your husband talks about how everything you do, everything you say is so that someone will view you as some kind of savior."

Cecily found herself breathing more deeply than she thought humanly possible. It was all she could do to stand there without lunging for Karen's neck. And Karen sensed the anger rising up in her old friend and cautiously took a step back. But Cecily continued to step forward like a cat on the prowl. "Don't you ever presume to tell me about what my husband thinks of me. You may be screwing him, and I doubt that you're doing that well, but he is still married to me. He is not trying to leave, has demanded that we stay together; he will not walk out on his family, so everything that you are doing is in vain. At night, he comes home to me!"

"But when you kiss him, it's my snatch that you taste on his lips."

No more words were spoken; there was only one big bang as Karen's head was bashed into the soda machine behind her. The store greeter gasped and Cecily heard him call for help as she made haste to her car.

CHAPTER 32

Karen was lying on the hospital gurney waiting for Andrew to come and take her home. She had insisted that she was okay, but once the store manager saw a thin trail of blood flowing from the back of her head, he insisted on calling the paramedics. She was taken by ambulance to a local hospital where she was advised that she may have suffered a mild concussion. The cut on her head didn't even require a single stitch. Her pride had been hurt far more than her head.

Andrew stepped from behind the little curtain that separated Karen from the rest of the emergency cubicles. "Hey there... What in the world happened? Are you okay?"

"That woman you're married to attacked me. I saw the heffa in Wal-Mart and she went off."

"What did you say to her? It's not like Cecily to go off on anyone without provocation."

"Oh, so now all of this is my fault? Gee, thanks for the sympathy, Andrew." Even though she realized that Andrew knew she'd spoken in some foul manner, Karen played the victim to the hilt. She explained that she was only trying to be cordial and would never cross the line of being obscene because the situation was difficult enough as it was. The lies fell from her lips so convincingly that she began to believe them herself. "Look, it's been a trying evening, please just take me home?" Within a few minutes, the pair was heading out of the hospital and down the street to grab some Varsity burgers since Karen's detour prevented her from eating earlier.

Andrew escorted Karen into her apartment and was surprised to see Hannah there waiting for them. The look of concern on her face was a little shocking to Andrew. He had gotten the feeling lately that Karen was not one of Hannah's favorite people. He hadn't been able to pinpoint what their issue was, but he knew that the roommate's relationship seemed strained.

"Oh my goodness, Karen! Are you okay? What did the doctors say?"

"I'm fine; it was just a little bump on the head. Nothing major. I'm just in shock that Cecily had the nerve to lay her hands on me."

Hannah turned her back, but Andrew could still see her snickering. He couldn't get mad because it was quite funny to him as well. So far, Karen's mouth and behavior had garnered her two beat downs. He had no knowledge of the ass whooping Hannah had also administered. He had to wonder why she actually found their relationship worth all of this trouble. The sex was good, there was no denying that, but he'd made it clear that he wasn't leaving his family. For that reason alone he couldn't understand why she was so willing to hang on. But he was very willing to take all that she had to offer and it was his hope that she'd eventually offer up Hannah on the same plate she served herself from.

ððð

Andrew eased in the house; half hoping that Cecily was asleep. The kids weren't due to return from Savannah until the next day, so tonight would be the best possible time to discuss what had transpired. It only took a quick minute to realize that his wife was wide awake and more than ready to share her side of the story.

"Have you been to check on your little whore?" Cecily asked causally as her husband eased his way into their bedroom.

"If you're referring to Karen, yes, I've checked on her. Luckily she didn't require any stitches. You realize that she could have pressed charges against you?"

"And you realize that I don't give a damn, right? She can't expect to go around saying such things to me and think that she'll walk away unscathed. No woman worth her salt would've let her get away with talking that kind of smack. But let me guess, your pretty little liar didn't tell you what she said, did she?"

Andrew could only stand there looking like a stupid deer caught in the headlights. He fidgeted and danced around like a child in desperate need of a bathroom. "I don't think she mentioned it."

Cecily shook her head at Andrew's obvious ignorance of the woman he was sleeping with. She filled him in on the crude remark that Karen made to her and watched as his expression displayed total acceptance and understanding of the actions that she'd taken.

"Andrew, do you love her?"

"I love you and I love my kids. That's who I love."

"How can you say that with a straight face? You're never here. You're screwing someone that was so dear to me and you make no apologies for it. Your children aren't crazy, they know that things have changed and I swear Rachel seems to be withdrawing from you more and more. If you loved us you would either do right by us or let us go."

"I have been doing right by you and the kids for years. You have a beautiful roof over your heads, drive a fine car, dress in designer clothes, and eat like kings. Do you know how many women would kill to be taken care of like this? But you're a smart girl, Cecily. You know that everything has its price, the fashion in which you live is no different."

Tears stung the corner of Cecily's eyes. If anyone had told her that this is what life with Andrew would become, she never would've believed them. "The price has become too high for me, Andrew, I want out. I make a decent living on my own and can support me and kids in a comfortable manner. Not to mention the fact that it would be healthier for them. For our children to grow up thinking that this dysfunction we now live in is the norm, for them to think that this is acceptable will prove to be detrimental to them later in life. This can't be the kind of relationship you'll want your daughter to mimic. I know that you would never want this for her."

"What I want is for both of my children to have the best of everything. You can't afford the best on your own and I don't give a damn how much people go around talking about 'the strong black woman', 'the strong single parent', one person can't be as stable and strong as a two parent household. You are my wife, you took that vow before God and man to be with me until death do us part and damn it, you will honor that vow."

"And you vowed to be faithful and to take care of me in sickness and in health. You haven't honored any of that. It's time for us to recognize that we can't make each other happy. We need to take steps to dissolve this sham of a marriage so that we can both move on. Please… let me go?" Cecily was on top of the bed on bended knee and hands clasped in front of her literally begging for her freedom. Andrew was not moved.

"Are you a dog now? Stop begging…"

"You're right; I don't have to beg for a damn thing. I'm petitioning your ass for divorce tomorrow."

"And by the time you leave the attorneys office I'll have full custody of my children and all your shit will be outside on the curb. The choice is yours."

CHAPTER 33

Promises, that's all that Rhonda had given Roy when it came to introducing him to her friends or the possibility of moving their relationship to the next level. But she realized that he'd now grown tired of those promises and that she would have to step up to the plate if she wanted their relationship to continue. She'd very hesitantly picked up the phone earlier and made dinner plans with Cecily and Mama Shirley. These were the two most important women in her life and it only made sense for them to be the first to meet Roy.

Despite the fact that Rhonda was an excellent cook, it wasn't something that she did very often. Being a single woman and working so many long hours, she didn't really see the point. It was much simpler to stop by one of her favorite restaurants and grab something to go. But today she would take the time to prepare something special; cedar planked salmon, baked potatoes, asparagus, and her famous apple walnut cobbler for dessert. Her mouth was watering just thinking about it. She grabbed her car keys and purse and dashed off to the store to purchase all of the necessary ingredients. Roy would be arriving much earlier than the others, so she knew that she needed to get in and out of Whole Foods in a hurry. Rhonda certainly didn't want to have the man lurking outside the house waiting for her to return.

Cecily and the kids had decided to spend the night with her mom the night before. She had been so disgusted with Andrew and his refusal to separate that she couldn't bear the thought of being around him. He'd picked the kids up earlier in the day and taken them out for fun and games at Chuck E. Cheese's. When he dropped them back off at home, he'd promised Cecily that he'd be back for dinner and that declaration was all the incentive she needed to pack up and leave for the night. Naturally her mom welcomed them in with open arms, and after the kids were down for the night, mother and daughter had a good ole fashion heart-to-heart. Cecily shared with her mom the incident that occurred in Wal-Mart and the subsequent talk she had with Andrew regarding her desire for a divorce. But what she wanted to share more than anything was her relationship with Carter. She'd cleared her throat, opened her mouth, but couldn't bring herself to speak the words. She was too afraid of seeing disappointment in her mom's eyes. Despite the problems she and Andrew had, and regardless of what he did, her mom would fully expect for her to behave like the faithful, Christian woman she raised her to be. Cecily ended their conversation and headed to bed. She would have to keep her secret a little longer.

Both Cecily and her mom were surprised by Rhonda's dinner invitation. When she'd told them that she had someone special she wanted them to meet, they were floored. Mama Shirley had had many talks with Rhonda about her unwillingness to share her heart, her life with someone special. She understood that Rhonda hadn't had the best example of a loving relationship growing up, but urged her to use that example as a how to guide of what not to do and what not to accept from the one she loved. Mama Shirley hated seeing the beautiful young woman that she considered a daughter, set herself up for a lifetime of loneliness. Yes, this was a welcome invitation, it signified that maybe something Mama Shirley said had finally resonated with Rhonda and that she was now willing to give love a try.

Rhonda pulled in her driveway and Roy pulled in right behind her. She'd hoped to have a few moments to start dinner and straighten up before he arrived, but he wasn't going to give her that opportunity. She knew that he wanted to lend a helping hand and as much as she wanted to do everything alone, she decided to just go with it. Within minutes, he had the groceries in the house, unpacked and was anxiously waiting for instructions on what Rhonda wanted him to do next. Over the course of the next two hours, they cooked, cleaned, and laughed as if they were an old, happily married couple.

"Hey, Mama Shirley!" Rhonda gushed as she opened the door for her guests. "Hey, Cecily, y'all come on in." She exchanged hugs with everyone as they entered her home. "I hope you guys are hungry, I've made a ton of food and I don't want left over's cluttering up my fridge," she teased.

"Now you know we all brought our appetites and these kids will destroy anything that looks like a left over," Cecily cautioned. She opened her mouth to continue with her next statement when Roy stepped around the corner and took his place at Rhonda's side. Cecily's mouth closed and her eyebrows went up.

"Everyone, I'd like you to meet Roy. Roy this is my best friend Cecily, her mother, Mrs. Meadows, and her children Rachel and Brian."

"Hello, it's so nice to meet you." Roy stated nervously as he shook each person's hand. He knew that these were the folks closest to Rhonda and if they didn't approve, she wouldn't hesitate to take a step back from the relationship that they were building.

"It's a pleasure to meet you too, Roy." Mama Shirley gushed.

"Yes, it's good to meet you, Roy." Cecily finally added.

"Okay guys, let's head to the table and prepare to enjoy this hopefully delicious meal."

"Oh, I'm looking forward to this. You're an excellent cook and it's rare that I get to enjoy a meal that I didn't have to prepare," Mama Shirley stated as they all moved to the dining table and took their seats.

Roy and Rhonda placed serving bowls and platters full of scrumptious dishes in the center of the table. Everything looked and smelled delightful, everyone was anxious to dig in. "Mama Shirley, would you do us the honor of blessing the table?" Rhonda requested.

"Of course, darling shall we all hold hands." Everyone took the hand of the person next to them and Roy gave Rhonda's a little extra squeeze. From the corner of his eye he could see a little smile play at the corners of her lips. He wasn't the only one that noticed it. "Dear Lord, we come to you today with thanksgiving in our hearts. We thank you for the love of family and friends, old and new. We thank you for the blessing of good health, prosperity, and the knowledge and acceptance that you and you alone are our God and that all blessings flow from you. We thank you for this wonderful meal and for the hands that prepared it. Please bless it for its nourishment to us and for our service to you. These things we ask in Jesus' name. Amen."

As the food was being placed on everyone's plate and they began to eat, the conversation began to flow. "So Roy, you'll have to forgive me if I hit you with a barrage of questions, but my mind is flying and curiosity is killing me," Cecily began. Roy chuckled and gave her the green light to ask away. He had nothing to hide and welcomed the opportunity to get to know his woman's friends. "May I ask where you are from? You've got a strong southern drawl."

"You would be correct; I'm from Birmingham, Alabama." Roy went on to share with them how he moved to Atlanta ten years ago to pursue his career as an architect and how he and Rhonda came to meet. It didn't take long for Cecily and her mom to realize why Roy was the man that had been able to draw Rhonda into a real relationship. He was very open and forthcoming, funny, and seemed to be an all around good guy. But what was more obvious than anything else was his love for Rhonda. The way he looked at her, spoke about her, and interacted with her spoke volumes.

Three hours later the dishes were empty, their bellies were full, and Cecily had to prepare to leave so that the kids could get to bed on time. Tomorrow was a school day and without the proper amount of sleep, she would have two little monsters on her hands. Goodbye hugs and kisses were exchanged and then everyone was on their way. Everyone but Roy. As soon as the door was closed, he took Rhonda in his arms and began to kiss her passionately. She happily returned his affections. More importantly, she was completely satisfied with the decision to move forward with their relationship and allow herself the opportunity to fall in love.

CHAPTER 34

Unable to concentrate, Karen decided to leave work early and head home. Her plans to get pregnant hadn't worked out at all. She'd practically raped Andrew when she knew she was ovulating and nothing. She couldn't understand how these irresponsible teenagers could get knocked up in the blink of an eye, but those that had the means to actually take care of a child and desperately wanted one seemed to have so much trouble conceiving. She'd hoped that this would be a successful alternative to her original plan, but sadly it appeared that it was no longer an option. And without a child, there was no way that Andrew would consider leaving Cecily. The thought of his precious kids being raised in a broken home was unimaginable to him. When she'd pointed out how many parents had been able to successfully co-parent without being married, he'd demanded that she not ever bring the subject up again. If she did, he assured her that it would be the last time she'd see him.

Karen walked in the apartment looking for Hannah. She didn't see her car in the parking lot, but was hoping that she'd just overlooked it. She hadn't. She plopped down on the couch and started to contemplate the best way for Hannah to follow through with her original plan to get rid of Cecily. She'd truly wanted to find another way, but after Cecily's little Wal-Mart attack, she no longer gave a damn about having her dead and gone. The only problem was that she would be stuck with Cecily's kids for at least fourteen years. It all seemed like a hell of a price to pay to be with the man that she loved, but at this point, no price was too high.

Finally Hannah came walking through the door. "Where have you been? I've been sitting here waiting on you for the past two hours."

"And hello to you too, Karen."

"We need to talk..." Before she could finish her statement Hannah threw her hand up and walked off. Clearly she had no interest in listening to anything that Karen had to say. "Hannah, do not walk off when I'm talking to you. We have plans to make and damn it, you will hear me out." Hannah stopped in her tracks and turned to face the woman that she was convinced was mentally impaired.

"What do we need to talk about, Karen? I've already paid my half of the rent and my share of the utilities. I'm rarely here so that you and Andrew can have all the private time you need. What else could there possibly be?"

"Come and sit down." Hannah didn't move. "Hannah, would you please come and sit down?" Reluctantly, Hannah granted Karen's request and took a seat in the chair opposite her. "Look, I know I came up with an alternate plan to get Andrew away from Cecily, but it's not working. It's been a couple of months and I'm still not pregnant. It's time for us to move forward with my original idea."

"I will not cause that woman any harm, she hasn't done anything to me. Quite frankly, she hasn't done anything to you either. Karen, she was your friend, from what I understand she was really there for you during and after your divorce. Where is your loyalty? And more importantly, once she's gone what makes you so sure that it'll be you that Andrew chooses to be with?"

"Of course he'll want to be with me, he wants to be with me now. It's just that this whole broken family thing has him stuck. Trust me, if Cecily were out of the picture, he would be begging for my hand in marriage."

"You sound delusional." Hannah stood up to leave but Karen grabbed her by the arm and snatched her back down.

"I may be a lot of things, but crazy is not one of them. I know without a shadow of a doubt that Andrew will be my husband once Cecily is out of the picture. And despite how you feel about the situation, you will be the one to take her out. I am sick of hearing your refusals and arguments. We both know that you're going to do it because the alternative is unacceptable to you. So I suggest you get comfortable with all of this because it's going to happen and I mean soon."

Hannah dropped her head and began to shake it in disagreement. "You know I can't do this, I can't take an innocent woman's life. She has children and they need her.

They are far too young to have to grow up without their mother." With tears now rolling down her face, she thought of the options that had been laid out before her. "I can't do it, I won't do it."

"Just so you know, I have every detail of your life. I have your family's information and everything else that the cops will need to track you down and toss your ass back in prison. I have detailed notes on our visits, or lack thereof, and I have the sworn statement of the woman you attacked and threatened with a gun."

"What the hell are you talking about? I don't have a gun and I certainly haven't attacked anyone."

"That's not what my records show. Brandy Haynes signed an affidavit stating that you punched her in the face and threatened her with a weapon. You realize that it's a felony for an ex-con to have a gun in their possession?"

"Who the hell is Brandy Haynes?" Hannah screamed.

"She's the lovely young lady that owes me a big favor. Now I'm going to go to my room and relax for a while, it's been a stressful day and I'm a little tired. While I'm gone you should think about your decision. Is Cecily's life worth more to you than your freedom?" Karen stood to her feet and sashayed off as if she didn't have a care in the world.

For the life of her, Hannah could not understand what she'd done to deserve this, couldn't comprehend how she'd gotten herself caught up in this mess. She cried as she weighed her options and finally decided that there really was no choice, she simply refused to go back to prison. She didn't have the strength to survive that again. With her mind made up she called her mother to tell her what was going to happen.

"Hannah, you can't do this. I'm going to come down there and together we can figure something out. There has to be a way to put a stop to Karen. We've got to find something on her that will force her to let go of this insane plan and leave you alone for good."

"Mom, she has so much information on me, a phone call from her could land me in prison damn near the rest of my life. She has covered all of her bases."

"Maybe she has, maybe she hasn't. Either way, I'm coming down there and we're going to get you out of this mess."

CHAPTER 35

The three weeks since Carter and Cecily had seen one another seemed more like an eternity. Although they talked constantly, the conversations couldn't compare to seeing each other face to face. So when Carter suggested that they sneak away for a mid-day lunch break, Cecily readily agreed. She informed her manager that she had an afternoon appointment and would return to work the next day. Carter gave instructions to his employee, grabbed his satchel, and headed out the door.

There was a great little southern café tucked away in the corner of a strip mall not too far from Cecily's office. She stopped in and placed an order to go for one of their favorite meals, grilled chicken with baked potato and steamed broccoli. She didn't know if Carter had plans for them to go out and eat, all she knew was that once she got to his place she didn't want to leave until it was time to pick her kids up from their after school program. She didn't have to wait very long for the food and within the hour she had pulled up in front of Carter's place and was carefully taking the bag of food out of the car. She didn't notice the white BMW that was parked in the drive across the street. She moved up the walkway towards the front door when the person in the BMW recognized her and got out to speak, but he stopped short when he saw Carter walk out and welcome Cecily with open arms. The guy watched intently as the love birds kissed hello and stepped into the house.

The voice of an angel was playing softly through the speakers. It was one that Cecily had never heard before. "Sweetness, who is that singing?"

"It's Eva Cassidy. She was a great songstress, one of the most beautiful voices I've ever heard."

"You said 'she was,' is she no longer living?"

"No, she passed away some time ago from cancer. Seems all the good ones die young." Carter leaned against the counter watching Cecily as she moved about the kitchen, placing food on plates and filling glasses with Ginger Ale. He admired her beauty, loved her quirkiness, and desired her body. The longer he watched her, the less interested he became in the food she was serving.

"Come on Mr. Everton, let's sit and eat this food while it's still warm." Dressed in one of Carter's white tee shirts, Cecily moved across the room with the plates in hand and carefully placed them on the table. Carter was hot on her heels with the beverages she'd poured. They sat and ate and shared great conversation about their families, their youth, and what they each hoped for their future. And just as Cecily thought she couldn't be any more attracted to Carter, he'd say something that would draw her in even more. Something that would make her heart beat with a little more love.

Their meals were half eaten but neither was as interested in the food as they were each other. They cleared the table and Cecily began to try and clean the dishes, but Carter could no longer control himself, he pulled her away from the kitchen and led her to the bedroom. He laid her down and immediately moved to the treasure between her legs to partake of the sweetest dessert. His tongue danced in and out of her love and licked her into a mind blowing frenzy. When he rose up and moved to enter her, all she could think was that she wanted to make him feel as good as he'd just made her feel. She sat up and with him standing she was in perfect position to take his full manhood into her mouth. She moved back and forth, taking him in over and over again. When he felt that he'd explode, he repositioned them so that they formed a perfect sixty-nine. They each licked and sucked one another to perfectly satisfying orgasms.

Lying in each other's arms, Cecily marveled at how their hearts seemed to beat in unison. This is how she felt it should be all the time. Not stuck with someone that you barely tolerated, but in love with someone that accepted you, listened when you spoke, and was willing to do whatever was necessary to make you happy. This was what she wanted for the rest of her life. But one glance at the clock and she was yanked back to her reality. She had to get ready to leave; her children would be ready to head home soon. She kissed her lover passionately and started to crawl out of bed, but he stopped her and kissed her again and again. She wouldn't leave until after they'd made love one more time.

ððð

The phone rang and Andrew reluctantly picked up the receiver. "This is Andrew."

"Hey man, what's up?" Andrew immediately recognized the voice of his brother Steven.

"Dude, it's been a while since I've heard from you, how have you been?"

"I've been good, just working hard and trying to stay out of trouble. But man what I want to know is why didn't you tell me that you and Cecily got divorced?"

"Divorced, why in the world would you think we were divorced? You know I don't believe in that mess, once mine always mine."

"Oh…my mistake, forget I said anything. What's been going on with you? Have you talked to Mom lately?"

"Come on now Steven, you know I'm not going to let you off the hook that easily. What made you think that Cecily and I were divorced?"

"Man I'm not trying to start any mess and I certainly don't want to cause problems in your marriage. I thought I saw Cecily today but I was obviously mistaken. My bad, like I said, forget I said anything."

"Where did you see her?"

"Come on man, let's just drop it."

"Steven, please just tell me where you saw her?"

"I was over at my girl's house and I thought I saw her going into the townhouse across the street."

"Who was she with?"

"She arrived alone but there was this tall, slim dude already there. I assume it's his house."

The more Andrew heard the angrier he became. "How long was she there?"

"When I left two hours later she was still there."

"Okay…alright… Well Steven I'm going to have to run. It was good talking to you and we will definitely hang out soon."

"Alright Andrew, please remember that many times things are not what they seem. Keep a calm head about yourself, man. Later…"

"I hear you Steven. I'll catch you later." Andrew disconnected the call, grabbed his briefcase and headed out the door. As he drove home, thoughts of his wife banging another man danced in Andrew's head. He tried to shake the thoughts, but they wouldn't subside. The idea of her doing to another man what she'd done to and with him was almost more than he could take. He whipped his car into the drive and jumped out like he was ready to kill someone. The way he burst into the house startled not only Cecily, but the kids as well. His entrance immediately killed all of the fun and laughter that was being shared between his wife and his children.

"What in the world is the matter? You burst through the door like a mad man." Cecily looked at him with a face etched in confusion.

Recognizing that he'd scared the kids, Andrew decided to temporarily tuck his anger away and calm himself. "It's been a long, hard day. I didn't mean to scare you guys. Rachel and Brian, daddy sure could use a big hug."

Without hesitation, Brian took off running into his father's arms. Rachel on the other hand, moved slowly and methodically. She embraced her dad, but not with the same enthusiasm as her brother. A brief hug around his neck and she backed right off. Rachel was young but as her grandmother often said, she had an old soul. She knew that there were problems between her parents and without provocation from her mom she'd decided that whatever the problem was, it was all her daddy's fault.

Andrew picked his things back up and headed upstairs without any further acknowledgment of his wife. The way he breezed past Cecily let her know that his attitude went far beyond a long, hard day; it was all about her and something she'd done or said that he was pissed about. And of course, she was clueless as to what it could be. What she did know was that she wasn't pleased with his storming in and blowing the natural high she'd had from her afternoon with Carter. But since Andrew had taken his bad attitude upstairs, Cecily decided to put whatever could be wrong out of her head and continue enjoying her time with her babies. When they saw her lighten back up and start to tease and play with them again while they prepared dinner, their anxiety immediately disappeared, especially Rachel's.

Upstairs, Andrew paced back and forth across the bedroom floor. The more he thought of Cecily with another man the more he could feel a storm starting to stir within all over again. He began to undress when he spotted Cecily's purse. He snatched it off of the dresser and rifled through it until he found her cell phone. He couldn't help but think how stupid she was for not using its lock feature. Within a minute he had scrolled through all of her calls looking for unfamiliar or frequently used numbers. Nothing jumped out at him. It was no surprise to see Rhonda's number over and over again, they talked and texted one another constantly. The fact that Rhonda had two separate numbers listed didn't faze him, he assumed that one was for work and the other her cell. The reality was that one was her cell and the other was Carter's. And quite naturally, she erased all text messages from the number that actually belonged to Carter. Exasperated, Andrew placed the phone back in the inside pocket of her purse, but as he placed it back his fingers brushed against something else, a key. He pulled the key out and examined it closely, it wasn't their house key nor was it Mama Shirley's house key. In that moment, he decided to drop the attitude and not confront Cecily once the kids were asleep like he'd originally planned. In the span of two minutes he concocted an entirely new scheme that he knew would get him the confirmation and answers that he was seeking.

CHAPTER 36

The kids bounced down the stairs all bright eyed, bushy tailed and ready for school. Cecily had their breakfast prepared and waiting on the table. Fortunately, they weren't too hard to please and a healthy bowl of oatmeal was quite satisfying to them both. Rachel ate at a record pace and huffed and puffed in an effort to make her big brother hurry up as well. Today was Field Day at her school and to say that she was excited would be a huge understatement. Finally, everyone was done eating and they headed out the door, but to Cecily's surprise, her SUV was gone. Andrew inexplicably took her car and left his Acura for her to drive. She didn't have time to call and question him, she just tossed her and the kid's bags in the passenger seat, checked her children's seat belts and took off.

Taking a detour from his normal route, Andrew pulled into the parking lot of the Spy Shop. The business was owned by a friend of his and he often referred clients who were looking to gather information on someone else to the store. "Byron, what's up man?" Andrew asserted.

"Nothing much, surprised to see you here. What brings you to this side of town?"

"I need a favor. I need you to equip my SUV with one of those small GPS devices that will track its whereabouts."

"You mean to tell me that you don't know where you're going or how to get back there?" Byron laughed at his own little joke.

"Very funny… This is my wife's car and we're going through some things right now. I was told that she may be cheating on me and I've got to know for sure before I make my next move."

"Oh wow, Andrew, that's pretty deep man, but I'm sure the second hand information you got is false. Full of untruths man, full of untruths."

"I hope you're right. But with this little GPS I'll know for sure. I can't turn a blind eye and be made a fool of."

It only took Byron two minutes to place the little device underneath the car and another three to explain how it worked. He told Andrew how he could track the cars movement via his cell phone. It could not have been simpler and Andrew was anxious to return the car to his wife and see where she's spending her free time. But he calmed himself realizing that if he went and swapped out cars now, it would raise a red flag with Cecily. She didn't question much but by no means was she stupid. Andrew was already surprised that she hadn't called him demanding to know why he switched cars without giving her prior notice.

"Alright Byron, I really appreciate this. You've been an incredible help."

"No problem, but you know that most cell phones are equipped with GPS and you could have tracked her for free with your service provider."

"True, but then she'd be able to track me as well. That's why we have separate cell phone accounts and I plan to keep it that way," Andrew chuckled.

Byron scratched his head and groaned. "That's why I'm single. Marriage brings entirely too much drama. I hope you get the answers you're looking for, man. Take it easy."

"I'm sure I will. Thanks and I appreciate all the help. I'll catch you later." Andrew walked out the door and headed to his office.

The evening was uneventful, Cecily never bothered to ask Andrew why he switched vehicles, she knew that chances were he'd just start spewing lies. She got the kids off to bed, took a long, hot shower and fell into bed. Andrew on the other hand gathered his things and left for the evening. His absence didn't faze Cecily at all, she'd come to appreciate having the king sized bed all to herself.

Waking refreshed, Cecily got the kids off to school and she took off for work with a smile on her face. She'd gotten an early morning text from Carter inviting her over after work. A quick call to her mom to ensure that she could pick the kids up and everything was set. Knowing what was waiting for her at the end of the day, she was able to breeze through her work and maintain her joyful mood. As happy as she was, she couldn't ignore the fact that the clock seemed to have been ticking very slowly. But finally 4:00 arrived and Cecily sprinted out the door. To her great pleasure, Carter was waiting for her at the front door. She dashed into his arms and that's where she stayed for the next two hours.

Andrew activated the GPS as soon he was awakened that morning. He'd periodically checked his phone for activity, but Cecily's car hadn't moved all day. It was parked at her job and that's where it stayed…until 4:00. Andrew assumed that his wife was on her way to pick up the children, but to his surprise, she headed out towards Buckhead. The GPS alerted Andrew of the location where the car had been parked and when he looked up the address he saw that it was a town home belonging to a Carter Everton, all he could think was '*got you, bitch!*'

CHAPTER 37

The jeweler that was thrilled with the commission he'd make from the sale of the three carat engagement ring he'd just made to a tall, handsome young man named Carter. It had taken Carter two hours to pick the perfect ring.

"Are you going to pop the question tonight?" The jeweler inquired.

"Oh no… The situation is complicated so I'll have to carefully choose the time and place for the proposal. She's a very special woman. I don't want to scare her off but I need her to know that I am totally committed to her."

Across town, another jeweler smiled his approval at the five carat princess cut diamond that Roy had chosen. In his heart, Roy knew that Rhonda was worth more than the cost of any ring that he could ever purchase. He hadn't discussed marriage with her, but he had told Rhonda time and time again how much he loved her. She knew that there was nothing he wouldn't do for her. He loved her smile, her sense of humor, her ambition, and she was the most beautiful woman he'd ever laid eyes on. He still wasn't sure how he was able to attract and hold on to such an amazing woman.

"Have you decided how you're going to propose?" The jeweler quizzed.

"I have and while I'd like to put on a big production, a lot of hoopla wouldn't be appreciated by my future fiancé. She's more subdued and likes to keep things nice and simple."

"Well over the years I've learned that it's best to propose in the manner that you know will be most comfortable for your intended. Take a woman out of her element or trying to do some big public proposal is a quick way to get her to say no. You'd be surprised at the number of women who say yes to a public proposal, but as soon as she's alone with the guy she says no."

"I certainly don't want that to happen," Roy chuckled. "Besides, I want her to know how important she is to me and I don't think I can properly convey that at a stadium full of people." The pair shared a laugh; Roy thanked him for all of his help and took off. His confidence was shaky, but he was praying that Rhonda would agree to be his bride.

He'd waited four days and the anticipation of her reaction was killing him. If Roy could hold on just a little while longer, he'd have his answer and he was praying that it would be yes. He'd arranged for Rhonda to meet him for dinner at one of her favorite place, The Ritz-Carlton's Atlanta Grill. What she didn't know was that he reserved a private room just for the two of them. The room was beautifully decorated and Roy had them place bouquets of roses all around the room. Music from

Rhonda's favorite jazz artist, Chris Botti, was piping through the speakers. The atmosphere couldn't be more perfect.

An hour later Rhonda walked through the doors of their dining room and was stunned by the beautiful décor, flowers, and music. Roy greeted her with a hug and suddenly she felt butterflies. "What is this all about, babe?"

"It's all about us having a special evening. It's about you being deserving of the best of everything."

The couple laughed, talked and enjoyed an incredible meal. The empty dishes were cleared away and replaced by dessert spoons. But the waiter was instructed to delay the crème brulee for a few moments. Roy wanted to take this opportunity to pop the question. "Rhonda, you know that I love you. You know that I would move heaven and earth to make you happy. I can no longer imagine my life without you. I know that you've been hesitant to give your heart away, to really let yourself love someone freely, but I think that it's time you take a chance on someone. I want you to take a chance on me." Roy pushed his chair back and knelt down on one knee. He gently pulled the ring box out of his pocket and lifted the top to expose the ring. "Rhonda, would you please do me the honor of being my wife?"

Rhonda's eyes darted between the ring and Roy's hopeful face. Her silence seemed to go on forever and then finally she spoke. "I can't accept your ring right now, Roy; I need a little time to think before making a decision. Is that okay with you?"

Despite the words coming out of his mouth, his face couldn't hide his disappointment. "Of course, I know that this is a lot to take in and it's a life altering decision. Take all the time you need, but in the meantime I want you to keep the ring. Maybe it'll help you come to the right conclusion." Roy placed the ring on her finger and gently kissed her hand.

CHAPTER 38

The Hartsfield-Jackson International Airport was packed. Jesse now had a full understanding of what it meant to navigate your way through the busiest airport in the world. She shook her head in dismay as she watched the other frustrated travelers wait in security lines that seemed to stretch on for an eternity. Once she finally found her way to baggage claim, she wondered how much longer she'd have to be bumped and knocked around by people grabbing for their luggage before her mid-sized bag would finally come around. Ten minutes later she had her luggage and was rolling it out to curb with the intentions of hailing a taxi, but to her surprise, her baby girl was waiting for her with a smile.

"Hi Mom!" Hannah couldn't hide her excitement, she hugged her mom tightly until the security guard warned her to hurry and move along. She waved at the guard, letting him know that she would comply. "I can't believe you're here, finally I have an ally in this town." Hannah beamed as she tossed her mom's bags into the trunk of the car and whisked her off towards her apartment.

"How did you know that I was coming to town? This was supposed to be a surprise you know."

"Then you need an assistant that knows how to hold her tongue. As soon as I called to speak with you, she told me that I'd be able to talk to you in person because your flight would be in this afternoon. She immediately gave me all your travel details, even the hotel you were booked in, but I figured you could save that money and stay with me at my apartment." There was a hopeful tone in her voice, but it was quickly doused.

"Sweetheart, I don't think that my staying at your place is a wise idea. I don't think that I'd be able to hold my tongue or be responsible for my actions if I have to spend any time around that Karen."

"I knew it would be a long shot, but just thought I'd ask anyway."

"But I'd love to see where my baby girl lives. How about we go to your place, you show me around, and then gather some of your things and come stay with me at the hotel?"

The smile returned to Hannah's face. "That sounds like an awesome plan." Hannah maneuvered through the rush hour traffic and her mom couldn't believe the constant start and stop of the crowded highway. "I know that you're not used to this, but despite the traffic, Atlanta really is a great place to live. I can't wait to take you site seeing tomorrow. There are so many great landmarks, attractions, and museums to show you. Who knows, you may even be persuaded to move down here."

"Keep dreaming… We both know that that will never happen. I am firmly and forever planted in Missouri. And in all honesty, I didn't really come for a vacation or weekend of leisure; I came to figure something out with this mess you're in. I want to meet this Karen and see if there is some way to get her to abandon this insane plan she's concocted."

"I don't know, Mom. This woman is clearly unstable and there is nothing worse than an insane person with power."

"Oh but there is and that's a mother protecting her child."

It was another forty-five minutes before they arrived at the apartment. Just as luck would have it, Karen was about to enter the residence when they pulled up. "That's her, that's the infamous Karen." Hannah pointed towards the top of the stairs. Jesse watched Karen intently as she unlocked the door, crossed the threshold to the apartment, and closed the door.

"She doesn't look crazy to me." Jesse grunted

"Wait until you hear her talk, I promise your opinion will change," Hannah retorted. She grabbed her purse from the backseat and they ascended the stairs to the apartment. As soon as Hannah opened the door she could hear Karen's footsteps rushing towards her.

"Hannah, time is running…" Karen stopped cold when she realized that her roommate was not alone. "I'm sorry; I didn't realize that you had company."

"Karen, this is my mother, Jesse Graham. Mom, this is my roommate, Karen."

Karen extended her hand. "Hi Ms. Graham, it's so nice to meet you. I wish Hannah had told me you were coming, I would've straightened up a little."

"Please, call me Jesse. It's nice to meet you; Hannah has told me so much about you. I feel like I already know you and everything you're about." There was no warmth or kindness is Jesse's tone or handshake. The coldness in her greeting did not go unnoticed by Karen, and she began to wonder just what had Hannah told her mom about her. Surely she wouldn't be crazy enough to share Karen's intentions for Cecily.

Karen eased her hand from Jesse's grip. "I wish I could say the same, but Hannah rarely speaks about her family. Hopefully your visit will give me the opportunity to get to know you."

"I doubt it." Jesse then turned her attention to her daughter. "Darling, why don't you show me around and then gather your things so that we can leave?"

Hannah gave her mom a quick tour that ended in her room where she began to toss a few things in an overnight bag. She gathered her personal hygiene items, work clothes, and a few other miscellaneous things and announced that she was ready to go.

"Hannah, I'm going to be here for a few days. Don't you think you'll need more than what you've packed? I expect for you to stay with me at the hotel for my entire visit."

"I'm ready to get out of here. We have a lot to catch up on and I can always swing by here tomorrow and grab more clothes. Come on, let's go." Jesse followed her daughter out of the room and hastily moved towards the front door.

"Hannah, do you mind if I have a word with you in private. I promise it will only take a minute?"

Before Hannah could answer, her mom interjected. "She may not mind, but I certainly do. I haven't seen my child since the holidays and I'm ready to get our visit underway. I'm sure you'll have an opportunity to speak with her soon. Goodbye Karen." Jesse held the door open for Hannah and they left. Karen was dumb-struck by Jesse's treatment of her. She didn't understand how someone could take such an instant dislike to her.

"Mom, did you have to treat her so cold? I know that you don't like her or what she's about, but I don't need the extra headache. It's difficult enough living with her and trying to get her to back off of her plans. Your behavior may add fuel to her crazy fire."

"Hannah, the first thing you are going to do is stop tip toeing around that woman. I don't give a damn about her feelings and will continue to treat her in a manner that I feel suits her behavior. I don't like her and I want her to know it."

Hannah knew that to continue this conversation was pointless, her mom hated Karen and that wasn't going to change. The fact of the matter was, Hannah hated Karen as well, but Karen had her over a barrel and she felt trapped in so many ways. Hannah initiated a lighter conversation as they drove through the city to their hotel.

"So Mom, think you'll want to carve out a little time for shopping?"

"Baby, I know that you want to move on to different conversation, and I can appreciate that. You've never been good with conflict and have always tried to avoid confrontation, but this is unavoidable. My priority now is to get that Karen woman to subtract you from her equation of insanity. Once that's accomplished, we can buy the world if you like."

Whipping the car into the hotel parking lot, Hannah couldn't help but chuckle. "Fine, I know once you get something in that pretty little head of yours it's impossible to get you to focus on anything else." In no time at all they were checked in and relaxing in their room. The stress of everything had Hannah physically and mentally exhausted. She slept like a baby while her mother began to plot and plan a way to get her out of Karen's clutches.

CHAPTER 39

Driving by the set of gated condos, Andrew found himself growing very angry. He wasn't angry at the man he suspected was sleeping with his wife, wasn't even angry with his wife, but at that moment he was angry with himself. He couldn't believe that he had let his wife's discretions push him to the point of driving past some man's house like a jealous little college girl. Disgusted with himself, he decided that there was a much more mature and hands off way to handle things. He punched the gas and got out of there.

Back at his office, Andrew picked up the phone and began to call a couple of his professional contacts. It was no more than an hour before one of the private investigators frequently used by the firm showed up in Andrew's office. "Michael, thank you for interrupting your day and coming over." Andrew greeted the short, rotund man with a firm handshake.

"Not a problem, Andrew, this firm throws me more business than any other. I'll always drop everything when you or one of the other partners needs my help. Now tell me, what can I do for you?"

"Let me first say that this is a very personal matter, it has nothing to do with the firm or a client."

"I completely understand and rest assured your privacy will be respected."

"I have every confidence that it will be. Now on to the matter at hand, it seems that my wife has a new friend. I know his name and address, but what I need is access to his house and the emergency code to get through the security gate at his subdivision."

Michael rubbed his hand over his head and sighed deeply. "Wow, when you call in a favor you sure make it a doozy. The security gate code is not an issue, but a key to the man's house, that's a pretty tall order."

"Did I call the wrong man for this job?" Andrew challenged.

"Of course not," Michael asserted. "This is just going to require me to step a little outside of the law, something I try not to do too often. But what the hell, I have a great lawyer, right?"

"Indeed. You're the best investigator around, there's no way I'd ever let you hang out to dry." Andrew gave the investigator a card with his wife's lover's name and address on it. "Michael, I hate to rush you but the sooner I get this access, the better."

"I understand and it shouldn't take me too long to recover it. You should hear from me within the week."

The men shook hands and gave one another the man hug with a pat on the back. As soon as Michael left, Andrew picked up the phone and had his secretary cancel the rest of his day. His next call was to Karen. "How's your work day going?"

"Hey Baby, it was okay but hearing your voice has made it considerably better."

"I need a favor."

"Anything!" Karen was so anxious to please.

"Leave work and meet me at the apartment." His tone indicated that he wasn't asking, but rather demanding.

"I would love that, but I have a client scheduled for this afternoon."

"You're going to choose a parolee over me? I'm hurt."

"Of course not, what was I thinking? I'll call them and reschedule. See you in about forty minutes?"

"Make it thirty, sexy."

It was as if Karen could see the devilish grin on Andrew's face and she gushed. "Okay, I'll be home in thirty." Karen called her client and changed their appointment. Then called her supervisor and fed him a lie about why she had to leave. She snatched her keys and purse from her desk and tore out of the office. Karen sped through the streets determined to get to the apartment and freshen up before Andrew arrived. She'd barely had time to slip into her chemise before she heard Andrew coming through the front door. She moved towards the front room to greet him, but before she could make it up the hall, he appeared before her. He looked at her from head to toe with a glare in his eyes that she hadn't seen before. She was caught between being turned on and being somewhat afraid. Andrew reached for his mistress, but instead of caressing her like she expected, he literally ripped the gown from her body. Shocked by his aggressiveness, Karen started to slowly back away, but he grabbed her, lifted her off of her feet and carried her to the bedroom. He didn't gently lay her down, but rather tossed her to the bed like a rag doll. "Andrew, what is going on with you?" Karen mumbled with confusion etched across her face.

"Nothing is going on, I just want you. I want you so badly right now." Andrew disrobed hastily, reached for Karen's legs and snatched her to the edge of the bed. There was no romance, no foreplay, he simply plunged his manhood into her body causing Karen to gasp for air. He did it over and over again. Andrew stopped only long enough to flip her over and pull her to her knees, taking her forcefully from behind. As he pounded into her, it wasn't Karen that he saw; it was his wife that he imagined he was punishing for her unfaithfulness. He released all over Karen, composed himself, and got dressed. He told her that he had to return to work. For the first time in her life, Karen felt like a dirty whore who'd been physically used for reasons beyond her comprehension. She lay on the bed and cried silently.

Driving back to work Andrew recognized that his treatment of Karen was despicable and undeserving. While he had no intentions of being with her long term, he did actually care for her. He realized that he never should have taken his frustrations for another out on her. He knew that he'd have to find a way to make it right with her. In the meantime, he'd send her a huge bouquet of flowers with a card of apology and hope that she'd accept that until he could apologize in person.

Two hours after his departure, Karen's doorbell rang. The delivery man from A Daisy A Day stood before her with the most massive flower arrangement that she'd ever seen. She took the flowers and tipped the man with a five dollar bill. Still in awe, Karen sat at the table in front of flowers and reached for the card that accompanied them. It simply read '*You deserved better and I'm sorry.*' A smile spread across her face and she reasoned with herself that no one was perfect, but at least Andrew recognized the error of his ways and was willing to apologize. Deep in her heart, the feeling of being abused still nagged at her, but her mind refused to acknowledge it.

CHAPTER 40

For the past three days Andrew had stalked around the house like an animal on the prowl, and clearly Cecily was his prey. He played with the kids and helped with their homework, but wouldn't utter a single word to his wife. When asked a question by Cecily, he would ignore her. When the kids mentioned Cecily, he would playfully change the subject. As they moved into the fourth day of this ridiculous behavior, Cecily decided that enough was enough.

Andrew entered the bedroom to prepare for work. Cecily took a seat on the bed and watched him move about the room. "Good morning, Andrew." She waited a moment and when there was no response, she stood up and blocked his path. "Good morning, Andrew. How did you rest last night?" Andrew didn't open his mouth, he simply shoved her out of his way. But Cecily wouldn't be deterred; she jumped back up, back in his face. "Andrew, what the hell is going on with you? Why do you refuse to speak to me?"

"Get the hell away from me." Andrew commanded through clenched teeth as he grabbed her by the shoulders and flung her to the floor.

"You need to pack your shit, Andrew and get the hell out of here. I have lived with your crap for far too long and I refuse to live in a situation where there is a constant threat of physical violence."

Andrew stood over her and gazed into her eyes with an enormous amount of disdain. "Tell me how long you've been screwing around on me."

Cecily scrambled to her feet. She was unable to hide the look of shock painted across her face. "What in the hell are you talking about?"

"My brother saw you going into some dudes condo. He says you kissed him and when he left the area two hours later, you were still inside this man's condo. Don't try to tell me he's lying because I swear if you do I will try my best to break your neck."

"Did your brother also tell you that the *dude* he saw me with is my cousin? Did he tell you that I was inside for half the day crying my eyes out because you've been screwing my so called friend and treating me like shit? Did he tell you that I begged my cousin to show me a way out of this crappy ass marriage, but all he could do was hold me while I cried?"

Andrew stood there dumbfounded; he had no clue as to how to respond. Everything Cecily said could very well have been the truth. He decided to err on the side of caution and offer a half hearted apology. He finished preparing for work and left without even saying goodbye to his kids. As he drove across town, he replayed Cecily's words over and over again in his head. Then the scene that his brother described took over. Steven had made the encounter that he witnessed sound very intimate. Andrew determined that the best thing he could do was reserve judgment until he was able to get into the condo and scope things out for himself.

Focusing on work was not something that Andrew had been able to do. He had wasted a good part of the day staring out the window of his corner office. He looked out over the Atlanta skyline but all he saw were images of his wife pleasuring and being pleasured by another man. A knock at the door snatched Andrew from his thoughts and back to the reality of his work office. "Come in."

Michael eased the door open and stepped into the nicely appointed office. "Hey there, I would ask you how are you doing, but the expression on your face tells me that you're troubled."

"Is it that obvious?"

"Indeed it is. What's going on with you, Andrew?"

"I confronted Cecily about her affair this morning. She denied everything, said that the guy she was visiting was her cousin. Supposedly he was lending a shoulder for her to cry on as she shared with him all the problems that we are having. Quite honestly, I'm not sure what to believe."

"Then maybe you need to hold off on this idea of visiting the condo until you sort everything out?"

"Absolutely not! A little tour through that condo will answer all of my questions. Please tell me that you have the key?"

Michael shook his head, displaying his reluctance to turn over the key. Deep in his heart he knew that nothing good would come of this. But despite his misgivings, he reached in his pocket and pulled out the silver key. "It wasn't easy or cheap obtaining this little piece of metal. The locksmith gave me hell."

"Yet you were still able to get it. I knew that you were the man for the job, and believe me, your efforts will not go unrewarded. I really appreciate this Michael, more than you realize." Andrew took the key, shook Michael's hand, and escorted him to the door. Feeling a little better about getting the answers he was seeking, Andrew decided that today would be a good day to smooth things over with Karen. Not to mention the fact that it had been several days since he'd had sex. He knew that whether she was angry or not, Karen would provide the physical satisfaction that he needed.

Andrew knocked on the door before letting himself into the apartment. Karen came around the corner and saw him standing there giving her the puppy dog eyes. She crossed her arms, turned around, and walked back to her bedroom. Andrew followed, confident that her apparent annoyance with him was just an act. Before she could plop down on the bed, he reached and gently pulled her by the arm. "Baby, I'm sorry. I should never have come at you like that, you deserve so much better. I stupidly took my anger for someone else out on you and I realize just how wrong that was. I swear I will never treat you that way again for as long as I live."

"Who were you angry with, Andrew?"

"Is that really important?"

"It is to me, now answer the question. Who were you angry with?" Karen demanded.

Andrew was a little surprised that she was taking such a hard stance. "I had just found out that Cecily may be cheating on me and let my anger for her overtake me."

"So let me get this right, you were angry with your wife, clearly wanting to hurt her, but instead you came here and took it out on me. I'm the woman that loves and cares for you and instead of respecting that, you abuse it."

"No, Karen, no... It was never my intention to use or abuse your love for me. You give me everything that no other woman has ever been able to give me. I'm crazy about you, Karen. I need you." Andrew stroked her face as he looked deeply in her eyes. He gently kissed her cheek. "I'm sorry." He then kissed her mouth and was satisfied that his words had their desired effect when she returned his kiss. He stroked her body ever so gently as he began to remove her clothes. All of her defenses were down and she allowed him to pleasure her in a way that he rarely did. She didn't stop him as he buried his head between her legs. In Karen's mind, this was something he wouldn't do if he wasn't truly sorry and if he didn't love her. She was all too happy to return the favor and give him all the loving that he could stand.

Holding Karen in his arms; Andrew began to share with his lover what his brother had told him. He spoke of how hurt he was at the thought of another man making love to his wife and the confusion he'd felt when Cecily offered her explanation of who the man was. Yes, he'd decided long ago to not ask Cecily any questions about her comings and goings and in turn, he didn't have to offer up any explanations of his own. He went on to say that he'd obtained the key to the condo where Cecily had been spotted. He'd use it to find out once and for all what his wife was doing and with whom she was doing it. Karen listened intently but kept her thoughts on the matter to herself. She actually hoped with every fiber of her being that Cecily was cheating. Her indiscretion could actually be a means to a happy ending for Karen.

Out of the blue, Andrew changed the subject by making the declaration that he was hungry. Apparently her loving was so good that it had caused him to work up quite an appetite.

"We could run and grab something at IHOP," Karen suggested.

"I'm really tired, honey. Why don't you go down the street and pick something up from one of the fast food places?"

Karen was a little put off by his request. She didn't understand why they couldn't simply go out together and share a meal. "Okay, let me put on some clothes and I'll be right back."

"That's my girl." Andrew gushed. "Look in my wallet and grab some cash, it'll be my treat," he boasted as if he were actually doing something big. Karen finished dressing and went to the dresser to retrieve his wallet. That's when she spotted the single key laying with the other items from his pants pocket. She assumed that it was the key to Carter's condo. Feeling as if she'd just struck gold, Karen slid the key into her pocket and left the apartment in search of food. A quick stop at Home Depot and she had her own copy of the key and the means to put her plan into action. It was time for Hannah to do Karen's dirty work and make Andrew a single man.

CHAPTER 41

Rhonda nervously tapped her nails on the restaurant table as she waited for Cecily to arrive. It had been a couple of weeks since Roy had proposed marriage and she hadn't discussed it with anyone. Instead, she'd been a nervous wreck, biting her nails down so low that they'd almost bled. Her co-workers had taken notice of her distant attitude and tense demeanor. It wasn't like her at all, but her strict policy of not mixing work with her personal life kept those most concerned from asking what the matter was.

Finally Cecily arrived. Although she was only five minutes late, for Rhonda it had felt like an eternity. Cecily plopped down in front of her wearing a smile as wide as the Mississippi River. "Hey there, sorry I'm a tad late, but you know I wouldn't be me if I wasn't late. How are you doing?" Without needing to hear a word from Rhonda, Cecily could tell that something was eating her up inside.

"I'm fine, how are you doing? If that big smile plastered across your face is any indication, you're doing great." The waitress came over and placed two glasses of water on the linen covered table. She sweetly asked if they were ready to order, but Rhonda kindly asked for a few more minutes.

"I can honestly say that right now I'm fine, but that same statement coming from you is an obvious lie. What's going on, Rhonda? You're as nervous as a long tailed cat in a room full of rocking chairs."

"You sound so foolish with all of your old sayings," Rhonda giggled. "But in all honesty, I do have a lot on my mind." She began to fidget with her napkin, debating with herself as to how much she would share with Cecily when it came to her reasons for being so hesitant to accept Roy's proposal.

"You know that I'm here for you, you can share anything with me. So come on and spill the beans."

"You know that I've been seeing Roy for a while now and things with us had been really cool. But recently, he threw a major monkey wrench in our relationship." Before she could finish explaining the situation, the waitress came back to the table inquiring about their food order. Rhonda told her through clenched teeth that they would need a little more time. "Roy proposed to me." She reached into her purse and pulled out the beautiful ring he'd purchased for her. She looked across the table to see her friend sitting there with her mouth gaped open in disbelief. "Well say something," Rhonda demanded.

"That has got to be the most beautiful ring I've ever seen. What did you say…did you accept the proposal?"

"I told him that I'd have to think about it. I tried to give the ring back, but he told me to keep it while I contemplate my answer."

"I'm confused, Rhonda. I know that you have really fallen for him and I know that he treats you like a queen and loves you very much. What is there to think about?"

Rhonda didn't want to make her best friend feel bad about her marital situation so the interruption by the waitress was a welcome one this time. The ladies gave a quick look at the menu and ordered an appetizer platter and a couple of salads. "You can't stall forever, Rhonda. The waitress is gone and I'm still waiting for an answer. A completely honest answer I might add."

"Honestly, Cecily the thought of marriage scares the hell out of me. My parents were a mess. Everyone thought that they were the perfect couple, but behind closed doors they were a mess. My father was a domineering bully. He talked to my mom as if she were the gum on the bottom of his shoe and didn't think twice about smacking her every now and then. My mom used to tell me about how happy they were before they got married and she advised me to be careful, said that marriage changed the happiness."

"That's not always true, Rhonda. There are plenty of happily married couples. They are who you need to look to as an example. You can't let yourself be jaded by the issues of other couples. I promise you, everyone's situation is different."

"How can you still say that with all the hell that Andrew is putting you through?"

"Yes…Andrew is putting me through more than any woman should have to deal with. However, Carter has come along and shown me that not all men are created equal. They are not all asses, they are not all selfish, and many of them still desire to put their women first. Roy is one of those men; all he wants to do is love and care for you. You need to trust that, Rhonda."

"That's easier said than done my friend." The food arrived and Rhonda wasted no time digging in. She hoped that the meal would occupy Cecily for a while and deter her from trying to convince her friend of all the glorious wonders of love. For Rhonda, actions spoke louder than words and all of the actions she was seeing in relation to marriage were horrible.

"How long do you plan to keep him waiting?" Cecily asked with a raised brow.

"As long as it takes for me to be one hundred percent positive that I'm making the right decision. Now tell me, how are things with you and Carter?"

"Things with him are great, Rhonda. He gives me everything I miss at home, reminds me constantly of what a relationship should be. I feel safe with him, cared for and protected. He makes me feel so desired and I swear I crave that man. My heart and my body literally crave him."

"Wow…that sounds pretty powerful."

"Isn't that what you want? Don't you think you can have that and more with Roy?"

"I do, but I'm scared to death that it would eventually fall apart." Rhonda admitted.

"You shouldn't live your life worrying about the what ifs. The saddest thing that can happen to a person is that they die regretting the chances that they didn't take."

CHAPTER 42

Despite the fact that Hannah whispered every word she spoke, her mother overheard the conversation anyway. Hannah wanted desperately to keep her mom out of the mess with Karen, but that was proving to be an impossible task.

"So that was Karen, right?" Jesse inquired.

"Yes, that was Karen; she was reminding me that the rent is due tomorrow."

"Really now? Most places I know require the rent to be paid on the first, not the eighth." Jesse looked at her daughter with one eyebrow raised and her head cocked to the side. This was the look she usually gave when she was waiting to hear the truth. She always did this to give her child an opportunity to clear up the lies that had just tumbled from her lips.

Hannah dropped her head sheepishly. "Karen asked to see me tomorrow, said that it was urgent."

"Baby, I don't want you jumping every time that nut case calls you. I didn't raise you to be some puppet on a string."

"You act like I have a lot of choices here. She has me over a barrel and I'm going to do whatever I have to do to stay out of prison."

"You are not a murderer and becoming one is the fastest way to ensure that you'll get locked up. What guarantee do you have that after you do what she's asking of you that she won't set you up and send you back to prison anyway?"

"There are no guarantees, Mom. But I know that my chances are better doing what she wants rather than not. And who knows, maybe I'll get over there tomorrow and Karen will tell me that she's changed her mind. For all we know, she may not even want Andrew anymore."

Jesse rolled her eyes sarcastically. "Yeah right, and dogs don't like bones."

Hannah couldn't help but laugh. Her mother was known for one-liners that were timely and always hilarious. "I swear I don't know where you get all these expressions from. But how about I just go see what she has to say and then we can figure things out from there?" It was the first time Hannah said anything about her and her mom working through this issue together, and quite honestly, she only said it to pacify her mom. She had no intention of involving her in any of this mess; she didn't want to take the chance of her mom being implicated in any criminal activity.

The next morning Hannah got up and headed out to class. She'd promised Jesse that she would come back and pick her up so that they could go to Karen's house together. She was prepared for her mom's anger because she had absolutely no intention of allowing her mom to be a part of that meeting. Unfortunately Hannah's time in class flew by. She loved learning about the human body and always became completely engrossed in her studies. But the time had come for her to head to the apartment and see what Karen so urgently needed to talk to her about. Hannah was surprised to see Andrew's car parked out front, he had never been around when Karen expressed how she wanted Cecily taken out of the picture. Certainly he wasn't now a part of this sinister plan.

As soon as Hannah stepped in the door, Karen rushed to her side and whisked her off to the kitchen. "My goodness, Karen what's the hurry?"

"I don't want Andrew to overhear us; in all honesty, I don't even want him to know that you're here."

Hannah breathed a small sigh of relief; she was glad that Andrew was not a part of this foolishness. There's no way she would've been able to change both of their minds or convince them of a better alternative. "Okay, I'll be as quiet as a mouse. Now tell me why you needed to see me?"

"Stop playing dumb, Hannah. You know very well why I wanted to see you. The plan hasn't changed, but it has been simplified."

"What do you mean by that?" Hannah's imagination was flying, only God knew what craziness Karen had concocted now.

"As luck would have it, Cecily is having a little affair of her own. Apparently she's been spending a good deal of time at her lover's condo. Andrew found out about it and was able to obtain a key to the place and the emergency code to the access gate."

"That's awesome!" Hannah could barely contain her excitement. "Andrew can catch her in the act and have all the ammunition he needs to win custody of the kids in the divorce. Then he and his kids will come running to you with open arms." Hannah thought she'd tied it all up in a neat little package with a bow on top. But of course nothing that made perfect sense to others ever seemed to work for Karen.

"Girl stop tripping, affair or not, Andrew is not divorcing Cecily. He has made that perfectly clear. He simply wants to put an end to the affair and that is not good enough for me. As long as she is around he'll never be free to marry me."

"So what hair brained scheme have you hatched now?"

"Hannah, I don't appreciate how you're talking to me. Your condescending tone isn't working for me at all. Now shut up and listen." Karen reached in her pocket and pulled out a key and a small piece of paper. "I took the opportunity to make a copy of the key and jot down the code. I want you to use them to get into the condo and take care of Cecily. You can hide out and wait for them or surprise them; I don't give a damn how you do it as long as Cecily ends up dead."

"Karen, do you ever think these ideas through completely? How in the world am I supposed to know when they'll be at the condo? What am I supposed to do with Cecily's lover? His identification of me would be more than enough to send me back to prison."

"I'm not going to tell you again about that damn sarcastic tone," Karen snapped. "Cecily has told Andrew that she'll be staying the night with Rhonda on Saturday while the kids are at a sleep-over. Of course she'll likely be with her side piece. All you have to do is get over there Saturday and carry out the deed. Now how you handle her lover, well that's your problem. I would suggest wearing dark clothes and a mask of some type. And for the love of God, don't drive your own car."

"Karen, I'm sorry for being an ass and speaking to you all sarcastic like, but there has got to be another alternative. Surely if you have a serious heart-to-heart with Andrew and tell him how strongly you feel about him, he'll voluntarily leave Cecily."

"Don't start kissing my ass now, Hannah. Don't you think I've told him how I feel, how much I love him? But his greatest concern is for his children and his desire to not have them come from a broken home. I promise you, Hannah if I had another choice I'd take it, but I don't. It has to be this way."

Tears rolled down Hannah's face as she took the key and slip of paper. Feeling completely defeated, she turned and left the room. With her head down she wasn't able to see that she was headed straight for Andrew. She bumped into his solid chest and looked up in surprise. "Oh…I'm sorry Andrew; I should've been paying attention."

"No worries. Hey, are you okay? Are you crying?" Andrew quizzed.

"I'm fine; I just have some things on my mind. I've got to go, y'all have a good day." Hannah rushed out the door, down the stairs, and sped away. She cried all the way to the hotel, trying unsuccessfully to compose herself before reaching her mom. She sat in the parking lot waiting for the tears to subside, but finally gave up after ten minutes of waiting. Hannah walked in the room, went straight to her mom, and shed an enormous amount of tears.

"Baby, what's the matter? What has you so upset?"

As she sobbed, Hannah recited the conversation she'd had with Karen. She explained how she tried to provide other alternatives, but Karen refused to entertain them. "Mom there is no convincing her that Cecily doesn't need to die in order for her to have a chance with Andrew. The crazy thing is, I'm almost positive that no matter what she does Andrew still won't choose to be in a committed relationship with her. He doesn't love her; he's just using her to fulfill his physical desires."

Jesse held her child and rocked her like she was once again a little baby that needed protecting. "It's going to be alright, Mom is here and I won't let you put your life, your freedom in jeopardy."

"But what choice do I have? She has left me no way out."

"Trust me, there's always a way out." Jesse assured her.

After Hannah made her hasty exit, Andrew turned his attention towards Karen. He walked over to her, grabbed her by the hair and pulled her head back. He kissed her deeply and let his tongue take a short journey to her neck. As he began to move back to her mouth, he made a brief stop at her ear and whispered. "This scene could be so much hotter if Hannah was a part of it."

"I thought I was all the woman you needed," Karen panted

"You are, but seeing you touch and kiss a woman as hot as Hannah would be an incredible turn on. I would go crazy if I were able to taste each of you, to have each of you." As Andrew spoke, he stripping Karen of her clothes and touched her body in a way that he knew drove her crazy. He continued trying to convince her as he sucked her nipples, one and then the other. "Don't you want to do this to Hannah?" He moved his hand between her legs and inserted his finger, in and out, around and around. "Can't you feel her touching you like this? You two can take each other to heights you've never known and then I can finish the job. I promise you won't regret it." He continued kissing and rubbing until he heard Karen utter the five words he didn't want to hear.

"Baby, that's not my thing."

As if he'd been doused with cold water, Andrew lost his erection and his desire to be with Karen. He stood straight up, pushed her away, and went to gather his things.

"Andrew, I know you're not going to leave me like this?"

With keys in hand, Andrew walked to the door. "Maybe another time." He walked out leaving Karen naked in the middle of her living room floor.

CHAPTER 43

Wednesday evening found Cecily and the kids at her mom's house for dinner and a little conversation. Cecily was beginning to feel a little run down and pulling double duty as mom and dad wasn't helping. Andrew's presence in the house had been pretty scarce and that meant that everything fell on Cecily's shoulders. Thank God for her mom, Mrs. Shirley had kicked in and helped with the kids more than usual during the last couple of weeks. She'd picked them up from aftercare, prepared dinner and helped with the kid's homework. Without a doubt, she'd be lost without her mom. It didn't matter that she was an adult with children of her own; Cecily wanted and needed her mom just as much as she did when she was a kid.

"That was really good, Mom. I haven't had your smothered pork chops in quite some time. And I know you gave me the recipe, but I swear you omitted something because mine don't turn out like that."

"That's because mine are made with an extra dash of love," Mrs. Shirley joked. "And we both know that you've never loved anything about cooking. It's something that you do out of sheer necessity."

"You got that right! If it wasn't necessary for me to feed those kids, I would seriously be eating fast food every day."

"And you'd probably be as big as a house."

"That would be okay, it would be more of me to love." Cecily smiled and then released a deep sigh.

"Baby, you're obviously tired. Why don't you go see Dr. Douglas? I know you hate them, but you probably need another transfusion. You can't go on like this, Cecily you've got to see about yourself before you pass out somewhere."

"I know you're concerned, but it's really not that bad. Besides, I have an appointment with him on Monday." Cecily had no intention of missing her already scheduled date night with Carter. As it was, she only got to spend time with him once, maybe twice a month. Not seeing him on Saturday simply wasn't an option.

"I hear you, but it seems that this weekend would be the perfect time. The kids will be here with me Saturday and if necessary I can keep them for the entire week. I just really want you to see about yourself." Mrs. Shirley got up from the couch and went to retrieve herself a cup of coffee. Cecily could look at her mom's posture and tell that she was deeply concerned, but she wasn't sure if all the concern was for her health. Mrs. Shirley walked back into the room carrying her favorite mug. It was the one that Cecily gave her for Mother's Day when she was ten years old. The daisy and words *Worlds Best Mom* had almost completely faded away.

"Mom, there's clearly something else on your mind. You're all hunched over and tense, a dead giveaway that something is eating at you."

Mrs. Shirley slowly sat down beside her daughter. She looked at her with loving eyes, as if she were already praying that the answer to her pending question would be a resounding *no*. "You're right; Cecily there has been something on my mind. Something I've wanted to ask you for a while. Are you having an affair?"

Cecily was momentarily stunned. This was a dirty little secret that she'd never wanted her mother to know. And although everything felt incredibly right about her relationship with Carter, in her heart she knew that she was wrong. "Mom, what in the world would make you ask me something like that?"

"It seems that every time I've kept the kids over night lately we haven't been able to reach you at home to say goodnight. If it's after eight, you can only be reached on your cell phone. You always used to treasure your time alone at home, but lately you seem to be running out the door as soon as you get a free moment."

"Mom it's a stretch for you to say that I'm having an affair simply because I've been going out with my girlfriends to blow off some steam."

"Cecily, I'm no fool. You've never been that gung ho about hanging out with the girls. If you went out once every couple of months, that was more than enough for you. And baby you are not at all stressed about your situation with Andrew anymore. The fact that he was cheating with Karen and treating you so poorly was driving you crazy. Now you don't seem to be concerned at all."

"I am very much concerned, but with his refusal to grant me a divorce there isn't a whole lot I can do. I've been speaking with my attorney and without risking him taking the kids away, all I can do is wait and hope that he screws up royally."

"Okay, if what you tell me is true and that's all that's going on then I apologize. But can I ask you to do one thing for me?"

"Sure."

"Turn and look me in my eye and tell me that you're not sleeping with someone other than your husband."

Cecily turned to look her mom directly in the eye. She'd never been able to look her mom in the face and lie and this was no exception. She didn't speak, but her eyes welled up with tears revealing the secret that she'd desperately wanted to keep from her mom. She dropped her head and allowed the tears to fall. She waited for the harsh judgments to come flying out of her mom's mouth, but instead she received a comforting hug. "I'm so sorry. I know that you expect more of me than this. I never meant to be a disappointment to you," Cecily sobbed.

"None of us are perfect, Cecily. As humans we are all flawed and all make mistakes. I'm not disappointed in you, I recognize that you've been dealing with a lot and not receiving the love you need at home. That being said, regardless of what you're going through, an affair is not the answer. It's time to correct that mistake."

"That's just it, Mom. This feels like anything but a mistake. Carter is a wonderful man and I've really come to love him. He treats me wonderfully, with love, respect, and true concern for my well-being. I know it's morally wrong, but it feels so incredibly right."

"Do you really think he loves you? He could just be taking advantage of a confused and hurt woman."

"He's not!" Cecily said defiantly. "While he's never told me that he loves me, his behavior speaks volumes."

"So this isn't something that you're trying to end anytime soon?" Mrs. Shirley sighed deeply, her concern etched all over her face. "What if Andrew finds out?"

"He won't, we're not careless and Andrew is so wrapped up in himself that I can't imagine he'd give a damn about what I'm doing. If he ever did find out I figure the worse that could happen is that he'd finally divorce me."

"Don't be naive, Cecily. Andrew would not take your indiscretion lightly. He is a volatile man and would be hell bent on making you pay for your disloyalty. Now don't get me wrong, I understand that he's been disloyal to you as well, but in his head you're supposed to honor your vows regardless of his actions."

"I hear you and I understand. I know you're right, Mom, and I will carefully decide how I proceed."

"That sounds like you're not ready to end this affair, but before you decide that for sure, please consider the repercussions for your children. They are the innocent ones and it's up to you to make sure that what's in their best interest is the driving force for all of your decisions.

CHAPTER 44

Friday night was date night for Rhonda. She was overly anxious to get home, shower, and dress for her evening with Roy. She'd worn his ring for some time now and had finally made her decision. Rhonda had prayed about it and sought council from her pastor, she was positive that she was doing the right thing. She turned on some music and danced around as she carefully selected her outfit. Hair done, make up on, and dressed in a beautiful sun dress, Rhonda looked in the full length mirror and was pleased with the reflection that stared back at her.

The doorbell rang alerting Rhonda of Roy's arrival. She opened the door and they greeted one another with smiles and hugs. "Hi, darling." Roy held her tightly and kissed her tenderly. "As always you look beautiful."

"Thank you… You look pretty good yourself. Now tell me, handsome, where are we going tonight?"

"How does dinner in New Orleans sound?" Roy asked with a sly grin.

"Oh stop playing, where are we really going?"

"I am serious, beautiful; I chartered a plane to take us over to New Orleans. It's only an hour flight, but we've got to get a move on, we have 8:00pm reservations at Andrea's."

"Oh my goodness, I can't believe that you've planned such an extravagant night. Let me grab my purse and we can leave." Rhonda was more excited than a fat kid with a sheet cake. In no time they were pulling up at the airport and boarding a private plane. The oversized executive chairs were beyond comfortable and the champagne was perfectly chilled. The giddy couple clinked their glasses together in a toast to the wonderful evening. The plane ride was smooth, almost as smooth as the limo that awaited them at the New Orleans airport. Rhonda felt as if she were staring in a romantic movie. Roy hadn't missed a thing; he'd pulled out all the stops.

The restaurant was beautiful and the Italian cuisine they'd dined on was beyond delicious. After a short car ride to the Riverfront, the couple walked hand in hand along the perimeter of the water. Rhonda stopped and pulled Roy closer to her as they listened to some of the local talent play a beautiful jazz song. Looking into Roy's eyes, Rhonda decided that the time was upon them. She could no longer walk around with this man's ring on her finger as if they were really engaged. She needed to share her decision with Roy; she knew it wasn't fair to keep him waiting. She slowly released his hand and timidly started to pull the ring from her finger.

"What are you doing, Rhonda, why are you taking the ring off?" Roy's face was becoming a canvas of disappointment. "Don't do this, don't turn me down."

"Roy, I've thought about this every minute of every day. I prayed about it and sought council to be sure that my decision was the right one." Rhonda placed the diamond ring in Roy's hand. "We need to do this properly, please ask me again, give me the chance to give you the proper response?"

Without hesitation, Roy dropped to one knee, took Rhonda's hand in his and spoke from his heart. "Rhonda, I love you. I've loved you for the longest time. I love how we speak to one another so openly and honestly. I love the respect we have for one another and how understanding we are of each another's careers. I've tried to imagine my life without you and I can't. You've become a part of me and I would be honored to be your husband. Rhonda, will you marry me?"

With tears rolling down her face, Rhonda spoke tenderly. "It would be my great pleasure and honor to be your wife."

Roy jumped to his feet and swept his fiancé up in a loving embrace. He'd gone from being scared that she'd say no to being overjoyed about their future as husband and wife. They were like school kids on a sugar high the entire flight home. The love they made once they hit Rhonda's front door was more intense than it had ever been before. The night had been nothing short of magical.

CHAPTER 45

Finally, the weekend had arrived and Cecily couldn't be happier. She'd taken the kids out for a Disney movie and pizza Friday after work. Cecily couldn't tell if they'd been more excited about wearing the 3D glasses or being allowed to eat dessert pizza. But one thing she was sure of, it was a great evening for the three of them and the joy she found in their happiness was unmatched.

The sun was barely up when Cecily heard pots and pans rustling in the kitchen. She rolled her eyes and shook her head in disgust. She was convinced that Andrew had made his way home and was on the hunt for food. To her pleasant surprise, Rachel was responsible for the noise. Cecily peaked around the corner to see her daughter trying to toast waffles and microwave bacon. She eased on into the kitchen and leaned against the counter. "Good morning, sweetheart. What are you doing?"

"Mom, you scared me!" Rachel exclaimed. "You can't be in here, you're ruining my surprise. Please go back to bed," she whined.

"Okay, pretend you didn't see me." Cecily hastily tiptoed out of the kitchen, back upstairs and jumped in her bed. Shortly after, Rachel carefully entered her mom's room carrying a tray of extra crispy waffles, brittle bacon, and orange juice. A wide smile crept across Cecily's face. "What do we have here?"

"Oh Mom, you already know, you saw me downstairs…remember?"

"I don't know what you're talking about. I haven't been downstairs."

Rachel cocked her head to the side and gave her mom a very familiar sarcastic smirk. It was the same face that Cecily used to give her mom when she was growing up. The one that said, 'you're so full of it.' Rachel sat the tray of food down in the middle of the bed. "Grandma's coming to get me and Brian soon and you'll be all by yourself. I wanted to do something nice for you so that you'll know that even though we're leaving you, we still love you."

"Oh baby girl, this is just about the nicest thing that anyone has ever done for me. Thank you so much." Just as Cecily reached for a napkin to dab the tears from her eyes, Brian stumbled in the room looking as though he wasn't quite ready to be up and about.

"What are y'all doing, do we all get to eat in our rooms today?" He reached for a piece of burned bacon only to have his hand smacked by Rachel.

"Brian, this is for Mom. Remember I told you that we needed to be nice to her cause she was gonna be all alone again." Cecily snickered at their sweet concern, offered each of them some of her meal and marveled at how they gobbled it up with no concern for the burned texture.

ððð

Jesse watched her daughter nervously tap her fingernails on the rim of her coffee cup. She had hoped that Hannah would get a good night's sleep and gain a clearer perspective on her current situation. No such luck, it had been more than twenty-four hours since Hannah had closed her eyes. Jesse had ordered her daughter a light breakfast, but Hannah pushed the plate away. The feelings of helplessness that hung over that hotel room were suffocating.

"I guess I'd better get ready and go." Hannah announced as she dragged herself up from the desk chair.

"Where are you going?"

"I have to go home so that I can get the final details for tonight from Karen."

"Fine, I'll get dressed and go with you."

"Mom, I told you that I don't want you involved in this mess. Just stay here and I'll be back soon."

"When I said I was going it wasn't a request. I'll be damned if I stay here while you plot and plan with a fool how to kill an innocent woman. I'll be ready in fifteen minutes."

True to her word, fifteen minutes later Jesse was dressed and waiting at the door. Hannah emerged from the bedroom and as soon as she saw her mom waiting for her, her face dropped in disappointment. It was her hope that she'd be able to sneak out while Jesse was still occupied in the bathroom. Her mom had never been on time for anything, but today she was ready, willing, and anxious to accompany her child on this outrageous mission. "You may as well wipe that look off your face and come on. You're obviously not thinking clearly, I'll be right by your side to serve as the voice of reason."

As they walked through the apartment door, the expression on Karen's face made it clear that she wasn't pleased to see Jesse tagging along. She greeted them in an icy cold tone and invited Hannah to step back to her bedroom so that they could speak privately. Hannah followed Karen just as she was instructed and Jesse was left to her own devices. She took the opportunity to look around the apartment, carefully studying the pictures of Karen's family and wondering what kind of fools they were. Jesse sashayed over to a corner table to get a better look at Karen's work identification and service revolver. All she could think was how stupid the government must be to have trusted crazy Karen with a gun. Jesse moved on to the other side of the room but somehow found herself drawn back to the table with the weapon and ID.

In the bedroom Karen was going over the details of the evening once again. Telling her how Andrew had planned to sit and wait at the condo for his wife and her lover to make their grand entrance. But it was Karen's plan to keep Andrew away from the condo and for Hannah to lay in wait instead. Once the couple showed up, Hannah was to use the small caliber gun that Karen pulled out of her dresser drawer to make sure that Cecily was removed in a body bag. "You still haven't explained what I'm supposed to do about her lover. I can't have him identifying me as Cecily's murderer." Hannah was near tears.

"Damn girl, do I have to tell you everything!" Frustration was oozing from every part of Karen. "Make sure you dress in all black, wear a hoodie so that your face is covered. There is no need for the guy to die, but if you shoot him in the leg or foot, it would distract him long enough for you to put a bullet through Cecily's heart and run like hell. Make sure you ditch the gun, preferably in a lake or sewer somewhere. The authorities aren't likely to find it in either of those places."

"She's your friend, Karen. You don't want to do this, she doesn't deserve it." Hannah tried her best to make one last convincing plea.

"I have no friends; females don't know how to be real friends. And every breath she takes keeps me separated from the man I want. He'll never completely be mine unless Cecily is out of the picture for good. Now take this gun and make sure you're at that condo no later than 8:00 tonight. Something tells me they'll be rushing back to get their freak on."

Hannah took the gun and stuffed it into her purse. She walked out of that room feeling more defeated and discouraged that she ever imagined possible. "Come on, Mom, let's go." Jesse glared at Karen with pure hatred in her eyes. She didn't offer any goodbyes, just followed her daughter out the door.

Just as she'd been advised, Hannah stopped at Wal-Mart for a pair of black jogging pants, black t-shirt, and black hoodie. Hannah cried silent tears the entire time that they were in the store and the entire ride back to the hotel. Jesse didn't know how to comfort her and knew that telling her to dump this insane plan was a waste of her breath. So instead, she passed her daughter tissues and gently rubbed her back. Once they settled in their room, Jesse ordered Hannah a nice pot of hot tea.

"Here baby girl, drink this." Jesse passed Hannah a cup of tea, sat down beside her and began to talk. She wanted to take her daughters mind off of what she was being forced to do. They reminisced about Hannah's childhood, how special her mom had always treated her and the wonderful experiences they'd shared. They laughed and for a while Hannah was able to escape her problems. Her mom had plied her with two more cups of tea, but it was okay, it was Hannah's favorite way to relax. Two hours after the laughter started, Hannah's mood began to take on that sad, serious, dark tone. It was time for her to prepare to leave. Jesse jumped up from the small couch they'd been sharing and went to the desk to pour one more cup of tea. "Okay, Hannah, I'm not going to try and stop you, but please just have one more cup of tea with me? Please, we may not get this chance again…please?" She begged and Hannah finally caved in to having one more cup. This one tasted a little differently from the others but Hannah didn't pay too much attention. She had bigger things on her mind. It was time to get dressed and go.

CHAPTER 46

Cecily had her overnight bag packed and waiting by the kitchen door. She was excited about her evening with Carter and was anxious to get it underway. She ran back upstairs to grab the pink, fuzzy handcuffs she'd picked up as a sexy joke for Carter. She bounced back downstairs and to her surprise, Andrew was walking through the kitchen and headed straight for her. She hurriedly jammed the handcuffs in her back pocket and covered the imprint of them with her shirt.

"You look nice, Cecily. Where are you running off to?"

"I'm going over to Rhonda's place. We decided it was time for a girl's night out. What are you doing here? I didn't expect to see you until Monday morning."

"I've been thinking…maybe it's time I get it together and come back home on a permanent basis." The truth was, Andrew had been doing a lot of thinking and knew that he was the reason that his wife was running off to another man. He'd decided that if he came home tonight and proposed that they work thinks out, he'd forget about her past transgressions. However, if she insisted on going out in spite of his attempt at reconciliation, he'd have no choice but to go to Carter's house and end their affair himself.

"Andrew, I don't know where this is coming from, but it's much too little and much too late. This marriage is beyond repair. The only reason I'm here is because of my children. I will never abandon them, even if it means being stuck in this hell hole until they're of age."

"Cecily, it's not too late to fix this. We are a family and family is everything. Our children will not be raised by a single parent; they will not come from a broken home. You know how difficult it was for my mom and how much my brother and I had to live without. I won't let that happen to our kids."

"How would that happen to our kids? We both make good money; they wouldn't have to go without a thing. And there are couples that have divorced and very successfully co-parent their kids."

Andrew's tone completely changed, it became deep and angry. "Damn it, that's not what I want. Now just stay your ass here with me so that we can work things out."

"Do you hear yourself? Making demands and treating me like crap is how we ended up so broken in the first place. I'm leaving… Rhonda is waiting on me and I need, no I deserve to enjoy myself. I'll see you tomorrow."

"If you leave, I promise that it's the last night you'll spend away from this house again. We are a family and we will remain a family."

"I'm leaving." Cecily knew that he meant every word that was coming out of his evil mouth, but she was not going to abandon Carter tonight.

"Well you enjoy yourself, but just know that this is it. I'll do whatever I have to in order to make sure that this is your last night away from me and your kids. Do you understand? Whatever I have to do."

Cecily walked to the kitchen, grabbed her bag, and headed out the door. The drive to Carter's place was bittersweet. She was so excited to see him, but knowing that it would be her last night with him was breaking her heart. The tears streamed down her face as she reminisced about all that they'd done, talked about, and hoped for. But none of that was to be, Cecily knew full well that if she didn't end things now, Andrew would make life more of a living hell than he already had. She couldn't risk having his rage towards her affect the health and security of her kids. Just before she reached Carter's house, she pulled over, wiped her eyes, and touched up her makeup. She didn't want to start their evening with tears.

As usual, Carter was waiting with open arms when Cecily arrived. He grabbed her bag and escorted her into the house. "You look amazing, baby. Tell me, what would you like to do tonight? We could go out and listen to a little jazz, shoot some pool, or check out the new exhibit down at Atlantic Station."

Cecily reached into her back pocket and pulled out the fuzzy handcuffs. She playfully swung them back and forth. "I thought we could stay in tonight."

"Bow chicka wow wow." That's all that Carter could manage to say in between bouts of soft laughter.

ððð

On the other side of town, the would-be assassin was dressed all in black and had removed the license plate from the car she'd be driving. While at the apartment she had handled the gun with a handkerchief, now she had on latex gloves. She had no intention of leaving her prints on the weapon. Nervously, she pulled out of the parking space and headed towards Carter's condo. The entire ride over she prayed to God for protection and forgiveness. What she was doing went against everything she believed in, but it had to be done.

She successfully made it past the security gate and watched as a couple backed their car out of their driveway a couple of houses down from Carter's. Once they were past the gate she pulled into their drive thinking that a car in a driveway wouldn't arouse as much suspicion as one parked on the street. She took a few deep breaths and was about to exit the car when she saw another vehicle park directly in front of Carter's house. She watched as he jumped out of his car and walked with a sense of urgency towards the front door. The tall, well built man didn't bother to knock; he pulled out a key and let himself in. He didn't bother to close the door behind himself. This could be her perfect opportunity, she thought she could slip in behind this guy and hide out until it was time for her to strike. She slid out of the car, eased up the drive, and into the house. But to her surprise, the man had a gun drawn, and was ready to kick the bedroom door down.

Cecily and Carter had made love and shared their feelings for one another. At that time, Cecily could no longer hide the truth. She confessed that tonight would have to be the last night that they'd share. As much as she loved Carter, she couldn't risk losing her children. Carter wiped her tears as he shook his head in opposition. "I told you, Cecily, this is not the end for us. I refuse to accept that you won't be a part of my life anymore."

"But Carter…" Before Cecily could finish her thought, the bedroom door was damn near kicked off of its hinges. Confusion ensued as a shot rang out in the night. Someone fell to the floor and someone else could be heard running from the house. Carter reached in the bedside drawer for his own weapon and flipped on the light. To their dismay, Andrew was squirming on the floor with a gunshot wound to his ass.

Gun drawn, Carter began to shout. "What the hell are you doing in my house?"

"Oh my goodness, Carter, it's my husband, Andrew."

"I don't know if I ought to call the cops or finish your ass off." Carter was furious and was more ready that he'd ever thought he'd be to pull the trigger and take a life.

Cecily scrambled to pull on some clothes as she tried to reason with Carter. "Baby, he's not worth it. I can't have you locked away over someone as pathetic as him. Please put the gun down." Cecily grabbed her cell phone and dialed 911.

Disgusted, Carter walked over and kicked Andrew's gun across the room. He didn't want to risk Andrew reaching for it and there being a shoot-out at the O.K. Corral. He then stepped over Andrew and cautiously walked through the rest of the house. There were no other intruders and one glance outside revealed that other than Andrew's car, there were no strange vehicles on his block. He did see a couple of neighbors peaking out their windows. "Nosy bastards," Carter mumbled. Just as he was about to step back into the house, the police arrived with sirens blaring.

After putting his gun down and convincing the cops that he was the victim, Carter escorted them through the house where they found Andrew still moaning and groaning. They assured Andrew that the ambulance was on the way and began to question everyone about the details of the evening. After hearing the events and searching the condo, a young cop returned with yet another gun and a work identification card. "Do any of you know a Karen Foster?"

"Are you serious?" Cecily asked in disbelief. Then she began to laugh… "Andrew, it looks like your lover girl followed you. While you were trying to get me she was trying to get you. Too bad for you she's a good shot." Cecily went on to tell the cops Karen's connection to Andrew and her.

Within minutes the ambulance arrived and sped off with Andrew. Cecily and Carter were asked to head to the police station to give a formal statement and a warrant was issued for Karen's arrest. Despite her love for Carter, this is exactly the kind of foolishness she wanted to avoid, wanted to keep away from her children. She knew that things could have gone much differently and was thankful to God that they hadn't.

CHAPTER 47

Feeling as if she were trying to find her way out of a thick fog of unconsciousness, Hannah turned and squirmed until she was awake enough to sit up. She looked around taking everything in and trying to remember the last thing she did. As she turned her head, her eyes fell on the black outfit from the night before. '*Oh my goodness, I'll be in jail before the day is over.*' The thought caused such anxiety that she began to have heart palpitations. Her eyes welled up with tears and she began to tremble.

Jesse walked out of the bathroom and saw her daughter looking like a scared little girl. "What's the matter, Hannah? Why are you crying?" She asked as she rushed to Hannah's side.

"Mom, how could you let me fall asleep and why didn't you wake me up? Damn it, Karen is going to have me locked up before the sun goes down." Jesse never replied to anything that Hannah said, instead she reached for the remote and switched the television to CNN. It wasn't long before one of the top news stories of the day was rebroadcast. The news anchor spoke about a husband's attempt to shoot his wife and her lover, but he himself was allegedly shot by his lover before he could fire his weapon. They showed a clip of local Parole Officer Karen Foster's mug shot and Andrew Connors limping into the police station in handcuffs. They went on to say that Andrew was arrested after being treated for a gunshot wound to the buttocks. Hannah starred at the television in a complete state of shock. "Mom, I don't understand. If she was going to try and kill Andrew then why bother trying to kill Cecily?"

"Hannah, you know that I would do anything for you, I'd protect you at all costs and that's what happened last night." Jesse continued to explain how she eased Karen's weapon and identification from the apartment and left them in the condo last night after shooting Andrew. "I never had any intention of harming anyone. I was simply going to fire a shot into a wall, leave her gun and ID, and run before anyone could spot me. But when I saw Andrew with his gun drawn and kicking down the door, I shot him where I thought it would cause the least amount of damage just to keep him from seriously wounding or killing the others."

Hannah leapt across the bed and hugged her mom so tight that Jesse thought she would stop breathing. Tears flowed down her face as she proclaimed her love. "Mom, you set me free, you freed me from the clutches of that mad woman. I love you so much, more than you'll ever know. How can I repay you for what you've done?"

Laughing, Jessie tried to pry Hannah's arms from around her. "You can repay me by loosening your grip."

"Oh, I'm sorry." Hannah released her mom and sat back on the bed. "Seriously Mom, you've saved my life. You saved me from another trip to prison, possibly a life sentence. I don't know how to thank you."

"You can thank me by living a good life. Finish your education, be a remarkable nurse, and raise a beautiful family of your own. Be happy, baby, be happy."

CHAPTER 48

Two weeks after the crazy scenario that played out at Carter's house, Cecily filed for divorce. Andrew was facing very serious criminal charges as well as disbarment. The power he once had over her was gone. Many of his fellow attorneys had turned their backs on him. Her lawyer advised her that in addition to receiving a great deal of the stocks and bonds, she should get approximately half of his retirement fund. All of that would make it possible for her and the children to remain in the house. The cherry that would top all of this off would be her ability to freely and openly spend an unlimited amount of time with Carter. They hadn't seen one another since the night of the shooting and Cecily was looking forward to the reunion that they would have in just a little while.

Mrs. Shirley prepared a fabulous Sunday dinner for Cecily and the kids. It wasn't Cecily's intention to eat as much as she did, but she simply couldn't help herself. The fried corn, fresh green beans, beef roast, mashed potatoes, and corn bread called her back for seconds and almost thirds. Cecily was thrilled to see the kids gobble up the vegetables as if they were eating candy. Once everyone had had their fill, Cecily cleared the table and washed the dishes. She kissed the kids and told them to behave and advised her mom that she wouldn't be long. Then she was off to Carter's.

Normally Cecily didn't believe in surprising people, but she thought today would be a good day for her to pop up at Carter's place. He was usually kicked back and relaxing on Sunday afternoons, so this would be a good time for them to celebrate her pending divorce. She was all smiles as she pulled up to the gate and found it open, she wouldn't have to call him to buzz her in. Cecily threw the car in park and practically skipped up the driveway. When the door flew open, Carter stood before her looking as handsome as ever. "Well hello there, sweetness. I thought I'd surprise you, make sure that you hadn't completely forgotten about me," she teased.

"Get in here, silly." As soon as she crossed the threshold, Carter greeted her with a warm embrace. They shared a very brief peck on the lips and Carter escorted her to the living room and asked her to have a seat. His tone was so serious that it made Cecily uncomfortable. She turned away from his stare in hopes of avoiding the devastating news that she felt was headed her way.

"Have a seat, love. Can I get you something to drink?"

Feeling her throat tighten and her mouth become dry, Cecily quickly took him up on his offer. "Yes, may I have a glass of water please?"

"Of course, make yourself comfortable and I'll be right back."

Cecily snuggled into her favorite spot on his couch and prayed that the sense of doom she felt was unwarranted. She looked around nervously and that's when she noticed the small ring box on the coffee table. She cautiously leaned forward and picked it up. She knew she shouldn't have opened it, but she couldn't help herself. Inside was the most beautiful engagement ring she'd ever seen. A smile settled on her face and she was instantly filled with a sense of calm and relief. No wonder he was so nervous, he was planning to propose. Cecily closed the box and tried to quickly replace it, but she wasn't fast enough. Carter caught her holding the box.

"I'm so sorry, Carter, I saw it sitting there and curiosity got the best of me."

Carter hung his head as he sat her glass of water on the table. "I'm sorry you saw that, if I'd known you were coming I would have put it away." He looked at Cecily and saw a look of confusion glaze over her face. He timidly sat beside her and took her hands in his. "Cecily, you know how strongly I feel about you; we've shared some wonderful times. Things were so amazing with us that I couldn't imagine you'd want to remain with Andrew. I had high hopes that your marriage would be dissolved and we'd be free to pursue a more serious relationship." Cecily began to have hope that her feelings of despair were misplaced, but that hope was short lived. "And I'm not saying that one day we won't be happily married, but that's a step that I can't take at this time. So much has happened, events that I never imagined I'd be a part of. It's all been a little too much for me. With that said,

I think that the best thing we can do at this time is to step back and try to regain a little perspective. I feel that a little space will help us determine where we really want to be, where we need to be."

Standing to her feet, Cecily wiped her tears and somehow found the courage to smile. "You're a great guy, Carter. All I want for you is happiness." She gave him a kiss on the cheek and knew in her heart that this would be the last time she'd ever see Carter Everton.

The closer she got to her car, the harder she had to fight to keep from breaking down. Her soul was silently begging Carter to come after her and tell her that he'd made a mistake, that he really did want her in his life forever. But he didn't, he just watched as she drove away. Her silent tears soon became a hysterical cry.

As if sensing something was wrong, Rhonda called but couldn't understand anything Cecily was saying through her heavy sobs. What she did know was that Cecily was headed back to her mother's house. Rhonda grabbed her keys and took off for Mrs. Shirley's. She arrived a few minutes before Cecily and told Mrs. Shirley that her daughter was heartbroken. They patiently waited for Cecily and as soon as she pulled up, Rhonda ran out to meet her. She held her friend until Cecily could compose herself; she didn't want the kids to be worried about their mom.

Mrs. Shirley sent the kids back to their play area in the back of the house and quickly took a seat beside her daughter. Initially no words were spoken; she just took Cecily in her arms and allowed her to cry.

"Go ahead and say I told you so," Cecily sobbed.

"Baby, I'm so sorry. I never wanted to see you hurt like this,"

"He was going to propose to me. I know that we never actually said the words, but I knew in my heart that he loved me just as much as I loved him and I was right, he did love me. But obviously that love wasn't enough."

EPILOGUE

It was amazing how much could happen in a twelve month period. Andrew was brought up on charges of assault, but the one friend that remained by his side got the charges reduced to second degree criminal damage to property. Andrew would be on probation for the next five years. Unfortunately for him, the one thing that he treasured more than his family was his profession and getting disbarred was a crushing blow.

Karen was stunned by her arrest and had tried desperately to convince the authorities that she'd been set up by Hannah. But with no evidence to support her accusations, they remained just that, accusations. Karen was convicted of aggravated assault and sentenced to four years in prison. She'd tried unsuccessfully to get Andrew to communicate with her. She wrote him, called his cell at every opportunity, and even left messages on Cecily's home phone in case he was back over there. Her mental state was fragile to say the least and she'd tried twice to take her life.

After witnessing Cecily's heartbreak, Rhonda nearly called off her engagement to Roy. She was not ready to be love road kill. But it was Cecily that reasoned with her, that told her that even though she was hurt in the end, she didn't regret one second she'd spent with Carter. "If nothing else, he showed me what I was missing and reminded me of how I deserved to be treated. You can't throw away a good thing because things didn't work out for me. Please understand that my relationship with Carter was doomed from the start. An affair is never the answer and I should have known that all that drama and the threat to his life was more than he'd ever intended to deal with. He's a great guy that did so much for my emotional state. I wish nothing but happiness for him and I wish that same happiness for you. Rhonda, you're an amazing woman who deserves the love of a good man. You have the man, now let him love you."

Rhonda followed her best friend's advice and married Roy in an intimate ceremony. She was a beautiful bride and she and Roy wasted no time expanding their family. It would only be another eight weeks before they welcomed their first baby.

After everything that had happened, Cecily decided that the best thing she could do was to devote herself to her children and her career. The time that she'd spent with the kids made all the difference in how they handled the divorce. She gave them a sense of security and they seemed to have found a peace that didn't exist when their father was bouncing in and out of the house. Cecily had also devoted a little extra time to cultivating her career. She'd completed a couple of training courses and was rewarded with a promotion and a nice bump in salary.

The one thing that Cecily wasn't interested in was a relationship. She was enjoying the satisfaction she found with her job and the new family life she'd established with her babies. So imagine her surprise when she found herself being wooed by a gentleman that occasionally had business in her office. For what seemed like the longest time, he'd asked for her number and she'd refused, he'd asked her out and still she refused. But his kindness, gentleness, and persistence finally won her over and she agreed to lunch. She figured it was a good start and was willing to patiently see if love or at least a beautiful friendship flourished.

Also in stores

Delphine Publications Presents

Her Sweetest

REVENGE 2

A NOVEL BY

Saundra

THE

Ultimate

No 4 No

TAMIKA NEWHOUSE

AUTHOR OF *KISSES DON'T LIE*

10-13

CPSIA information can be obtained at www.ICGtesting.com
Printed in the USA
LVOW07s1521101013

356370LV00002B/292/P